About the Author

David Lord is a preschool teacher from South Gloucestershire and an avid science fiction and fantasy fan. He dabbled in fan fiction and small writing projects for years but was encouraged to take on something bigger by several good friends. 'The Figment Wars' is his first novel.

For my mum and dad, to whom I owe my love of reading and fantasy and for my little sister, Natalie, who has shared in that same love of stories all these years and in the years to come.

David R. Lord

THE FIGMENT WARS:
THROUGH THE PORTALS

To Bethan

Imagine!

DPLord

AUSTIN MACAULEY
PUBLISHERS LTD.

A CIP catalogue record for this title is available from the British Library.

ISBN 978 1 78455 183 4 (Paperback)
ISBN 978 1 78455 185 8 (Hardback)

www.austinmacauley.com

First Published (2015)
Austin Macauley Publishers Ltd.
25 Canada Square
Canary Wharf
London
E14 5LB

Printed and bound in Great Britain

Prologue

Bogeymen do not exist. That is what parents have told their children for centuries. The problem with your parents telling you that something does not exist is that as soon as they have done so, your imagination conjures up exactly what the Bogeyman looks like and for the most fleeting of moments, you see him standing in the shadows in the corner of your bedroom. Shadows are indeed the natural home of the Bogeymen, and the fact that you could have sworn you saw one for that tiny instant is something that shall be explained when the time is right. Parents are quite right, of course. Bogeymen do not exist. Not in our world anyway.

Shadows are not only the home of the Bogeymen, but their exclusive network of travel. Flitting from one shadow to another allows them to travel vast distances in a matter of moments, with only a minimal risk of detection. Although it goes without saying that Bogeymen cannot stand natural light, it has been said anyway. The light paralyses them so; therefore, they avoid it at all costs. It is in the shadows that we find one particular Bogeyman making his way into the Impossible City at dusk, disappearing in one shadow and then instantly reappearing in another. His destination is a room in the Tower of Realms, a place he is most certainly not welcome. The citizens of the Impossible City despise all Monsters, but Bogeymen are hated even more fervently. This Bogeyman is a most horrid specimen of his kind, with wet, slimy skin, sunken grey eyes and a rotten, putrid stench about him. The man he is in such a rush to see, however, is fouler and infinitely more dangerous than any Bogeyman.

He travelled across the mind bogglingly large city, expertly avoiding the creatures who loath him and his brethren so much. Not just Bogeymen, but every other monster and foul thing are depending upon a successful venture. The outcome of the war depends on it. Before long, he finds himself in the courtyard of the Tower of Realms. Leering up at the lumbering structure, he can see the room he must flit into. Before he can do so, he heard someone approaching. He held his rattling breath and stood perfectly still. He watched as two guards wearing dark maroon uniforms pass by, their truncheons hanging at their belts. They soon moved further on and the Bogeyman flits again, instantly reaching the room he has been looking for. Hiding in the shadow cast by a large wardrobe, he waited, sensing the light getting dimmer and feeling more comfortable for it. Bogeymen are more disposed to move freely at night, but certain defences around the city would have prevented him entering any later than he did. He would be trapped there until dawn, but he knows his contact will keep him safe until the time comes to make his escape. After two hours of waiting, the door to the room opened. He waited to hear it close again, followed by the key turning in the lock, before stepping out of his hiding place.

'You're late!' he rasped.

'It could not be helped.' The man who had just entered swept across the modestly furnished room to a small table and cabinet, from which he produced a bottle and glass. 'I regret I have nothing to offer you in the way of refreshment,' he said lightly as he poured himself a glass of the bright purple liquid. He put down the bottle and gazed out the window of his chamber. He did not wish to look upon his guest if he could help it. He'd had far too long and gruelling a day.

'My brethren and I grow impatient!' snarled the Bogeyman. 'The war has already taken a turn for the worse since we moved so many of our troops. The accursed Heroes are advancing on all fronts!'

'Which is precisely what we wanted them to do, is it not?'

'They have gained too much ground already! The next stage must ...'

'Must what?' asked the man, stopping his glass halfway to his lips. The Bogeyman cowed instantly at the sharpness of his tone. The man turned from the window and looked at his revolting guest. Not a hard, cold stare, nor even an angry glare. He merely looked at him. 'Kindly do not presume to suggest at what pace I should proceed. The next stage is delicate, too delicate for you to even begin to understand. Many attempts have already been made without success, though each try brings us closer.'

The Bogeyman could only just about bring himself to look his contact in the face. The brash nature of his kind was at odds with his fear of what this man was capable of doing.

'I ...I have only been sent to convey our concerns ...our losses have been great ...'

'Your gains will be greater, after tomorrow,' said the man, casually taking a sip from his glass.

'Tomorrow? So soon? Really?' The Bogeyman could not help but smile, revealing crooked teeth as drool slid down his chin. The man drained his glass and motioned towards the wardrobe. He needed to pass on the message and take his leave, for he was expected elsewhere by more respectable company. The Bogeyman obediently crossed to the wardrobe and opened the door, knowing it would be a safe hiding place until dawn, when he could flit away again in the early morning shadows, undetected by the city's defences. He climbed into the wardrobe, ignoring the fact that his contact had taken up a perfumed spray bottle and was using it copiously. It was just about strong enough to cover the Bogeyman's foul odour. The contact then began to close the door, but held it open long enough to say one more thing before taking his leave.

'Come the morning, you will return to tell the others that the next stage is finally ready to proceed. By this time tomorrow evening, we will have precisely what we need to escape this world forever. A human child.'

Chapter 1

By the Woods

Thomas Llewellyn was at an awkward age, the age where you're not quite old enough to go on the holiday of your choice but too old to spend holidays visiting family you barely know. In Thomas' case, he was spending the school holiday visiting an aunt, an uncle and his nine year old cousin, Emily. Being fourteen, Thomas had little to nothing in common with his cousin. Then again, his ten year old brother, Isaac, had even less in common with Emily but not on account of his age. Thomas was of the opinion that school holidays should be an opportunity to spend less time with family, not more. Based on the fact that they had crammed the two boys into the car and driven for four hours to spend two long weeks with a set of incredibly dull relatives, Thomas' parents did not share in his opinion.

Aunt Kate and Uncle Norman's house was close to a wood. Merely yards away from their back garden. Thomas had vague memories of going off to play in that wood on a previous visit, years ago when Emily and Isaac were just babies. There wasn't much in the way of woodland where Thomas lived, and even if there were, he wasn't allowed to hang around in it. Thomas was sure he must have enjoyed exploring this particular wood once, but now it was just one of the many things about the place that made it all so very boring. More boring than Chemistry with Mr. Bolton and if you've never taken a Chemistry lesson with Mr. Bolton, just be glad of it. Thomas yearned to be older in the way only fourteen year olds can. When he became what is commonly known as 'older', he'd spend holidays with his friends and even go abroad with them. He knew this was the case because he'd seen it on television. He didn't yet know how he and his friends would pay to go abroad, but he assumed he'd have money when the time came. You could get a job once you turned sixteen, and Thomas assumed the job market was ready and waiting for young men like him. Fourteen year olds do a great deal of assuming when it comes to their future.

For the present, he was sitting in a deck chair, looking out at the wood that lay so close to his aunt and uncle's garden. A half-drunk glass of homemade lemonade sat on the garden table beside him. Thomas was used to brand names on everything, and having to pretend he liked Aunt Kate's concoction was another thing he hated about this visit. He looked out across the treetops that were twitching ever so slightly in the breeze, thinking of his friends back at home. What might they be doing right now? Hopefully they were as miserable as he was. Every last one of them. Not Ernie, of course. His parents had taken him to Spain for the holidays. Ernie was hardly likely to be miserable, and even if he was, at least he got to be miserable in a sunny climate. Thomas' thoughts were interrupted when his mother appeared at the door behind him.

'Thomas, have you seen Isaac?' she asked.

'Hmm?' he mumbled, though he had heard her perfectly the first time.

'Isaac. Your brother,' she said, knowing full well he had heard her perfectly the first time. 'He isn't anywhere in the house. Have you seen him?'

'Not since earlier.'

'How very helpful and specific. Well, you can go find Emily at least. She'll be where she always is, down by the wood. Tell her lunch is ready and see if you can find your brother while you're at it.' His mother promptly disappeared back into the house, leaving Thomas to force himself out of his seat and start the relatively short trek out of the garden and down to the wood.

Emily was nowhere to be seen as he approached the wood. She did have a habit of venturing in, and Thomas quickly deduced he would have to do the same in order to retrieve her. As he walked, he thought how few parents back home would allow their nine year old child to go off alone into the woods. It obviously didn't bother his aunt and uncle, as Emily knew the forest better than Thomas knew his own street. He trudged past the first few trees and started calling Emily's name. Getting no reply, he trudged in further, being especially wary of any weeds that looked like they might be poison ivy ...or was it called poison oak in Britain? Thomas couldn't seem to remember. He couldn't tell one plant from another anyway so it seemed best to just try and avoid them all. After walking past several trees that all looked the same to him and calling her name for what felt like the tenth time, he found Emily sitting on a large log, engrossed in a book.

'There you are! Didn't you hear me calling?'

'Sorry, I didn't hear you. The Duke is about to find out that his daughter has run away with a servant boy, but he doesn't know yet that his wife has been replaced by the Dragon Queen,' said Emily without looking up at her cousin. Her tone seemed to suggest that what she had said not only made perfect sense but was also a sound explanation as to why she hadn't heard him. Thomas didn't know his cousin all that well, but there was one thing he did know about her. She liked to read. Reading may have been just about all she ever did. Books of nearly every genre littered his aunt and uncle's house. Evidently her parents also enjoyed reading, so much so that they didn't actually own a television. This had greatly startled and dismayed both Thomas and Isaac, only Thomas was better at hiding it. Much better, in fact, as will soon be made clear.

'That's fascinating. Lunch is ready, so it's time to come inside.' Thomas turned as though to start back through the woods then remembered something. 'Oh, you haven't seen Isaac, have you?' Emily shook her head only slightly, barely disturbing her long brown hair or her concentration on her book. Thomas cursed under his breath as he'd now have to go looking for his brat of a brother. Still not taking her eyes off her book, Emily jumped down from the log and started walking slowly in the direction of the house. Thomas was scanning between the trees for any sign of Isaac.

'You don't like being here, do you?' asked Emily, still reading her book as she walked.

'What?'

'You and Isaac. You don't like being here with mummy, daddy and me.'

'That's not ...well, it's not really ...' was all Thomas could manage before Isaac appeared behind them, pushing his way roughly past some bushes.

'No, we don't!' he declared. Thomas and Emily both turned to look at him. His sudden arrival had even managed to break Emily's concentration on the fascinating story unfolding before her. 'There's no television, no Internet, no games, no nothing here! It's all so boring! The sooner we go home, the better.'

Thomas sighed, almost in disbelief. His brother was as obsessed with gadgets and games as it possible for a ten-year-old to be. Thomas had lamented the lack of an Internet connection too, but he just wasn't hot-headed enough to complain about it every second of the day. Isaac, on the other hand, made no secret of how much he was missing his favourite shows and online games. Thomas was most annoyed about how he couldn't update his online status while he was here, but then again he wasn't doing anything worth updating. Not yet, anyway.

'I told you. You don't like it here,' said Emily.

'I didn't say that, he did!' said Thomas, holding up his hands defensively.

'You're thinking it, Tommy!' sneered Isaac. 'You hate being in this stupid place with that stupid girl as much as I do.'

'Shut up, Eyes!' growled Thomas. The two brothers, like most brothers around the world, knew exactly how best to wind each other up. Knowing what name the other disliked being called was just a starting point. 'What are you doing out here, anyway?'

'Trying to see if I can find a signal, obviously!' Isaac screwed up his face as he said this, in a way that emphasised the freckles on his face. Everything about Isaac's features screamed 'Brat', or at least it did to Thomas. If his looks weren't enough, his behaviour confirmed what a consummate brat he was, as it was only now that Thomas noticed what Isaac was holding in his hand. His own hand dived towards his trouser pocket, only to discover it was empty.

'That's my phone! You nasty little ...' He lunged at his brother, but Isaac was too quick and managed to run around him. Emily merely sidestepped well out of the way of them both and then returned her attention to her book. Within seconds Thomas had managed to grab hold of Isaac and was wrestling him to the ground trying to wrench the phone from his hand. All three of the children, for we shall refer to them as children even though Thomas is fourteen and would object, were too preoccupied to notice the branches of the trees start to sway above their heads.

Even if they had noticed, they'd only have put it down to the wind. It might then have taken them a few seconds to realise that at that particular moment there was no wind, which might in turn have caused them to pay closer attention as the swaying of the branches became more and more pronounced. As we've already established though, they had not noticed because the boys were busy fighting and Emily was busy reading. Branches swaying is one thing, but when the branches of two trees sway towards each other and begin to grow longer and intertwine, someone is bound to notice. Isaac did indeed notice as he lay on the ground, pinned down by Thomas, who had finally managed to get his mobile phone back. Isaac's cry mingled with Thomas' triumphant shout at first, but when Isaac began pointing frantically at the branches rapidly wrapping around each other, Thomas looked up and saw it too. With the boys no longer fighting, the creaking of the branches could now be heard and Emily looked up from her book. Being possessed of a vivid imagination, she was intrigued by what was happening. The same could not be said for Isaac, who scrambled up from the ground in a blind panic, only to stumble and fall back down again. Thomas just froze.

The two trees had now bent towards each other, and the branches had become so tightly intertwined that it was impossible to tell which branch belonged to which tree. Indeed, the two trees now formed a kind of archway. It was only a matter of seconds after the branches had stopped moving that the wind picked up. The air stirred lightly at first, blowing in no particular direction, then quickly gathered strength. It also soon became much more focused, blowing straight towards the archway. Thomas held his arms up to his face as he struggled to stay upright. He tried to shout to his brother and his cousin, but he couldn't even hear his own words over the howling of the wind-like force. Leaves, twigs and dirt flew past his face and towards the tree arch. Unable to brace himself any longer, Thomas was brought down to the ground. He could feel himself moving along the ground, and with substantial effort he managed to roll over onto his back to see what he was moving toward. Once again, his words were drowned out, though this was just as well as they weren't pleasant.

The space between the two trees that had formed this arch had changed. Thomas could no longer see the rest of the wood that lay behind the trees. At first he thought he was looking at, quite literally, nothing. Sheer darkness had appeared inside the tree arch, though traces of other colours appeared here and there, swirling around the edges of the arch. It was then that Thomas realised that he wasn't being blown by the wind, but rather being pulled in by this vortex, like water going down a plughole. His hands scrambled at the ground, but there was nothing he could hold onto. Letting out one last, unheard cry, he was pulled close enough to the arch to be lifted into the air and into the vortex itself. The wood and the entire world disappeared from every aspect of his perception.

Chapter 2

Unhappy Landing

All at once, Thomas lost all sensation and feeling. Not only could he not feel his body, but he couldn't feel his mind either. All the panic he had felt back at the wood was gone. He didn't know it, but he was tumbling through the void between realms. He might have done so for a month, a year, but there was no way for him to know. As luck would have it, he was only crossing the void for a few seconds, not that time truly exists in such a place. If the void is truly a place. If it had not been for the power of the second portal pulling him through the void, Thomas himself would not have truly existed. All feeling returned to him in a rush as he fell through the portal and landed roughly on what felt very much like the ground. It certainly hurt enough to be the ground.

Disorientated and breathless, Thomas pushed himself up and tried to look around him. There wasn't a great deal to see. That's not to say there was nothing at all to see, like in the void, only that there wasn't much of interest to see. As his vision adjusted, Thomas saw that he had wound up in a barren wasteland. Dust and dark grey rocks made up the ground that had so roughly broken his fall. The sky above was even darker than the rock below. Thick, black clouds were spread across the sky with no sign of the sun. Thomas heaved himself up but being upright did not improve the view. Nothing but the same bare terrain as far as he could see. The only colour he could see was a small yellow and brown object a few yards away, which, as he got closer, Thomas recognised as Emily's t-shirt and trousers. Luckily she was still inside them.

'Emily, Emily! Are you ok?' he exclaimed as he rushed to her side.

'I think so,' said Emily as she sat up. Her voice was groggy, yet it still managed to contain that lightness that annoyed Thomas so much. 'What happened?'

'I really don't know …I don't even know where we are,' muttered Thomas as he looked around again, hoping to spot just about anything. He did manage to spot a familiar looking lump not too far away. 'Can you stand?'

'Yes, I'm just a little dizzy.'

Supporting her by the elbow, Thomas and Emily made their way over to where Isaac lay huddled and shivering. As they got closer, it became very suddenly obvious that the whole experience had affected Isaac worse than it had them. That was clear by the puddle of sick that was just too close to Isaac to be somebody else's. Being careful to avoid stepping in it, Thomas tucked his hands under Isaac's armpits and tried to heave his brother upwards. Isaac was hardly cooperative, becoming a deadweight the moment Thomas touched him.

'Come on, get up! Aargh! You bloody little …'

'I think we've left the country,' said Emily. 'This hardly looks like England.'

'That may be, but how?' grunted Thomas as he struggled to get his brother upright. 'Will you quit being so …come on, we shouldn't stay here.' With Isaac's arm across his shoulder, Thomas looked around again. Nothing had changed since he last looked, just moments ago.

'Which way are we going to go? Everything looks the same,' said Emily. 'Aren't we supposed to stay where we are, when we're lost?'

'Under any other circumstances, yeah ,' grunted Thomas, heaving Isaac up once again to stop him slipping. 'In this case, no, we don't stay where we are. For now we just get away from here. Try and figure out what this place is.' Choosing a direction at random, Thomas began to hobble, supporting his silent and sickly brother, out into the vast wilderness they had been dumped in. Emily followed close behind, still clutching the book she had been reading, her eyes wide with wonder rather than fear.

'It must have been magic,' she said extremely matter-of-factly as they walked along. 'What happened to the trees, and then to us, it couldn't really be anything else.'

'Don't be stu …silly,' said Thomas, remembering that he had promised to be kind to his cousin. 'Magic isn't real. Obviously something has happened to us, we just need to find out where we are, then we can …' The words dried up, in his mouth and in his mind. Not surprisingly, Thomas had no idea what they would or should do if they did work out where they were. Few adults would know how to cope with such an experience, so for a teenage boy and his nine-year-old cousin to be coping as well as they were was something of a marvel. Isaac had reacted the way most people would by puking up what remained of his breakfast.

They walked on for at least half an hour, Thomas having to stop now and then to shift his grip on Isaac, who showed no signs of coming to his senses anytime soon. The clouds above them had become darker, and sudden blasts of thunder could now be heard. Brief gusts of wind stirred up the dust, stinging their eyes and throats. During one of their stops, Emily suddenly pointed to the distance.

'Over there, look! I can see something!' Thomas hoisted Isaac up once again, so as to be able to stand up straight and see where Emily was pointing.

'I see them too …but what are they? Hills?' said Thomas, squinting as he tried to make out the distant shape.

'Whatever it is, it's something and it has to be better than nothing,' said Emily, gesturing around them, the book still in her hand. 'Let's keep going and see what we find.' The straightforward and casual optimism that seemed to be in every word she said was beginning to annoy Thomas. He wanted to drop Isaac and shout at the top of his lungs, rage against the world (though which one he was not yet to know) about the inexplicable and hopeless situation they had found themselves in. A rising feeling of sheer panic was lurking deep inside him, waiting only for his permission to surface and render him a babbling, swearing wreck. However, Thomas also had within him a rare sense of responsibility, and fate had decided that he was to protect his brother and cousin, irritating though they both might be. Saying nothing, he set his eyes on what he hoped were hills and started hobbling again, this time with Emily leading the way.

As they got closer, it became clearer that what they were headed towards were indeed hills. They looked just as barren and awful as the rest of the land around them, but where there are hills, there may be some caves or shelter of some kind. They had been walking for a considerable time, when Emily stopped, causing Thomas and Isaac to nearly collide with her.

'Emily! What is it now?' barked Thomas, losing almost all patience with just about everything. He could see that Emily was once again pointing into the distance. Between them and the hills, there was now a cloud of dust and grit. At the centre of that cloud was something kicking up all the dust as it came running towards them. Thomas couldn't be sure, but it looked as though there was more than just one 'something'. 'Hide,' he breathed. 'We have to find somewhere to hide, now!'

'There isn't anywhere to hide,' said Emily quietly. 'Maybe it's not …'

'Emily! We don't know where we are and we don't know what that is, so until we do we have to try and stay out of sight! This way!' Having nowhere else to go, he turned to his right and began virtually dragging his brother along with him as fast as he could. At first Emily stayed level with the boys, but Thomas urged her to go faster and not to worry about him or Isaac. Emily did so, but soon stopped again.

'There's something else over there!' she said, pointing out directly in front of them. Thomas looked up and his heart sank. There was indeed something else coming towards them from the horizon at great speed. When he looked back, he saw that whatever was coming from the hills had changed direction to follow them.

'Ok …ok …' said Thomas slowly as he put his brother down on the ground as gently as his tired limbs would allow. 'There's nothing else for it. We've nowhere to hide, we'll be seen if we try to run …so we stay here.'

'I did try to say, they might be friendly,' said Emily.

'Yeah, let's hope so …' The two of them sat down on the ground next to Isaac, trying to make themselves as small and inconspicuous as possible. Not an easy feat when all you have to obscure yourself is dust and small rocks. With each passing moment, the approaching figures got closer and closer. It became clear that whatever had come from the hills would reach them first. When they got close enough to be seen clearly, Thomas was struck with the feeling that they really should have kept on running.

Chapter 3

Caught in the Middle

Even if there had been somewhere to run to, there was no outrunning the terrible creatures that had come from the hills. An enormous grey wolf, bigger than any in nature, had come barrelling across the vast plain. Running alongside it was nothing like anything found in nature. More lizard-like than anything else, it ran on six powerful legs that had allowed it to keep up with the wolf. The children could see the dark purple plume coming from its fearsome, long snouted head through the dust. Its sharp, cruel teeth were surpassed only by the set of razors inside the wolf's own jaws. Both of these unnatural monsters had sighted the children, and doubled their efforts to reach them.

'Stay down,' breathed Thomas, 'whatever happens, stay down.' He raised himself slightly, looking around for anything he could use as a weapon. With only moments until the beasts would be right on top of them, he grabbed a small rock and held it firmly in his hands. The rock was the only sliver of a chance he had to protect himself and the others. The creatures would no doubt get them in the end, but he might at least take out an eye before he died, and going down fighting seemed better than begging or crying. He watched as the wolf and the lizard slowed to a halt. The wolf was breathing heavily and the lizard's tongue flickered in and out of its mouth. The wolf began to sniff the air and side step just a few yards away from the children. It intended to circle round them and size up its prey. Thomas decided not to wait any longer and hurled the rock as hard as he could, straight at the wolf. The jagged stone caught the wolf on the head but it barely flinched at the attack. A vicious snarl spread across its face and it took a step closer, its piercing eyes now focused solely on Thomas, or so it seemed to the now terrified teenager. His valiant attempt at a last stand had been futile. The wolf's sudden movement when it pounced barely registered with Thomas and what happened next took a moment or two to sink in as well.

Being so preoccupied with the obviously dangerous monsters bearing down on them, Thomas had forgotten all about whatever had been coming from the other direction. Emily, however, had not, and had noticed the half dozen men on horseback coming to what she assumed was their rescue. Her assumption turned out to be right, as one of the men managed to charge ahead of his comrades and thrust a great spear into the wolf just before it could attack Thomas. The man was nearly dismounted by the impact, but he steadied himself and his steed well and came around to face the wolf again. The spear had struck the wolf's flank. A yelp of pain was followed quickly by an enraged growl. The so far placid lizard-creature suddenly flared up, shaking its plume, hissing and spitting. It rose up on its back two legs, revealing long sharp claws on the remaining four feet. Thomas looked wildly at what he hoped was his rescuer. Everything about the large man and his horse suggested that they knew how to fight and had been doing so for a long time. In fact, the man was Thomas' perfect idea of what a warrior should be. Weapons of all kinds hung about his person and his chainmail armour was stained with dried blood. The consummate fighter and hero was ready to defend.

Not that he had to do it alone. The other five horsemen were soon on the scene, riding into position to surround their fearsome foes. The lizard lurched to the left and began swiping at the horses. Two horsemen pulled their steeds back to avoid the attack, their spears ready to strike. A third drew back an arrow in his bow, aiming for the beast's underbelly. The other three warriors were engaging the wolf, striking with arrow and spear and avoiding attacks by constantly moving. Thomas looked down to the ground at Emily and Isaac, the latter of whom was still showing no signs of stirring. The howls and hissing of the two beasts made it impossible for the children to be heard, even if they had anything to say to each other. Over the din, however, they heard a shout from one of the warriors, who was obviously more adept at projecting his voice in a battle situation.

'The sky! The sky!' was all he cried. Thomas and Emily looked up and saw a large black blur swooping towards them. Thomas threw himself to the ground and Emily quickly covered her head with her arms, being already down on the ground. A piercing shriek was added to the howls and hisses, followed by the sound of arrows being let loose. Thomas risked a glance upwards and saw a grotesque giant bat flying away from them, an arrow lodged in its side. Those fighters who had not fired on the bat did not allow their other adversaries to take advantage of its sudden arrival and pressed their attack. Two of the fighters charged at once and impaled the wolf on their spears. It let out a cry and shook itself wildly, dislodging the weapons. It began cowering and backing away. The lizard's hide was tough to penetrate, but the fighters seemed to know what weak points to attack, for it too had been stabbed numerous times. The bat flew around to try and dive at them all again, but it was met by another volley that it could not avoid. The lizard let out a strange, rasping sound and instantly it, the wolf and the bat all turned and began to flee back in the direction of the hills.

The archers fired a few parting shots while their comrades cheered.

'Captain Madroc, do we pursue?' asked one of the riders, pulling back on the reins of his wild-eyed steed.

'No, let the foul creatures go lick their wounds for now,' said Madroc, who now that Thomas' attention was drawn to him, did indeed seem the most commanding of the group.

'We're deep enough in enemy territory as it is.' As his men sheathed their weapons and calmed their steeds, Madroc turned his around so as better to see the children. 'Which only begs the question, what are you doing so far out here? Do you not realise where you are?' Standing up slowly, Thomas wiped dust from his eyes before looking up at Madroc. It had been Madroc who charged the great wolf first. He carried the blood soaked spear in one hand, and two swords were strapped to his back. A jagged knife hung from his belt. Underneath a dark red helmet, Thomas could make out shoulder length black hair. His glare alone would have been imposing enough without the multitude of weapons.

'Look …we don't want any trouble …the fact is we don't know where we are …' said Thomas, his voice hoarse from dust and thirst.

'Do you not indeed?' barked Madroc. 'I find that hard to …'

'Captain Madroc, with respect,' interrupted one of the fighters. Madroc turned his hard gaze upon the soldier. Thomas and Emily did the same, only their gaze was not so hard. 'I have heard tell of Friends who arrive dazed and confused, uncertain of who or what they are. Perhaps that is what has happened to these poor souls.'

'Possible, though it does not explain what they are doing so far out here. Friends never arrive in a place like this, so far from the Tower of Realms and they cannot have wandered so far from the city.'

'We weren't in a city,' said Emily, speaking up for the first time. 'We were in the wood outside my house. Something happened to the trees and …then we were here.'

Suddenly they heard a low groan, and even Madroc turned to look at Isaac, who turned out to be the source of the groan. He stirred and managed to roll himself onto his back.

'Isaac!' exclaimed Thomas, dropping to his brother's side. 'Isaac, you okay? Say something!'

'M …M …Mmm,' moaned Isaac.

'What is he trying to say?' asked Emily, peering at her pale, drowsy cousin over the shoulder of her other, slightly more alert cousin. 'Is he going to be sick again?'

'M …Mum …I w-want mum …' muttered Isaac, tears beginning to trickle from his eyes. He hadn't yet fully comprehended where they were or what they were facing, but he knew who could probably make it all better. Thomas, although grateful that his brother seemed to be recovering, couldn't help but wish that Isaac hadn't said that in front of all the big, tough warriors. As it happened, Madroc either didn't hear or pretended not to.

'We cannot stay here. The enemy may return in much greater numbers at any time.' Madroc turned in the saddle of his horse and shouted to his men. 'We ride back to the fort! Halor, Fendan and Kolat, these three confused Friends will ride with you.' He turned back to the children. 'You will come with us, and when we reach the safety of the fort we can arrange for you to travel to Impossible City. Someone there will be able to help you overcome your disorientation.'

'Dis …disorientation? What do you mean?' asked Thomas, standing up to face Madroc. 'Who are you people anyway? No …no, we're not going anywhere with you until I get some answers!' Needless to say, the pressure of all of this was becoming a bit much for Thomas.

'I fear you have little choice,' said Madroc grimly.

'I have one or two choices left!' shouted Thomas, scooping up another rock. Some of Madroc's fighters were laughing, but Madroc himself was far from amused.

'I salute your bravery, young Friend. Your other senses may be addled, but you have courage at least.'

'Where do you get off calling me 'friend'? I don't know who any of you are and I've got no reason to trust you!'

'Thomas …they did save our lives …' said Emily quietly, for she wasn't used to seeing her cousin like this. Then again, family visits being so scarce she wasn't used to seeing her cousin much at all. His whole body was shaking, yet the grip on the rock in his hand only grew tighter. So much so that blood had begun to seep through his fingers. Sweat threatened to blur his vision, yet his gaze did not leave Madroc.

'You'll tell us where we are or I'll …I'll …'

'You'll do what?' shouted one of the other warriors. 'Smite us all with your mighty stone?' This provoked further laughter. Thomas was now shaking with rage yet his grip on the stone remained firm.

'Enough of this. Olath, pass me some Sand,' ordered Madroc. The fighter who had spoken earlier began rummaging in a pouch on his belt.

'Sand? Sand!' exclaimed Thomas. He let out a hysterical laugh. 'You think I'll do what you say if you threaten me with sand? I've got to be …' Thomas didn't get to finish his sentence, as Olath had passed Madroc a small bag from his pouch. Madroc had emptied the contents of that bag into his open palm and then tossed said contents over Thomas. The second the Sand hit Thomas, he instantly fell into a deep and surprisingly contented sleep.

Chapter 4

Clothes in the Wardrobe

'Dreaming,' muttered Thomas, waking up slowly. Before his eyes were fully open, he could tell that wherever he was now, it was much more pleasant than where he had been before. He wasn't even sure he had really been where he was before in the first place. There is often that terribly confusing few moments after you wake up. The point where you're not sure if what you thought was a dream truly was a dream, or an absolute reality that you now have to deal with for better or worse. Thomas could remember being in his aunt and uncle's garden and then going to look for Emily. There had been a powerful gust of wind and dust. He seemed to remember a wolf and warriors on horseback. He shook his head vigorously, as though he could dislodge the images from his mind if he shook hard enough. He soon figured that he must have dozed off while he was sitting in the garden and that all the strange and terrible things that had happened since had been a nightmare.

The only problem with the notion that he had fallen asleep in the garden was that he had most certainly not woken up in the garden. Thomas had not fallen asleep in one place and then woken up in another since he was four years old. Neither his father nor his uncle could be considered strong enough to carry a fourteen-year-old boy. The biggest difference between this place and the garden was that it was inside. Walls were the biggest clue there. It certainly wasn't a room in his aunt and uncle's house. The thought struck him that he might be in hospital, but if so, how did he end up there? Of course there are several ways one can end up in hospital and none of them are pleasant. Thomas sat up slowly and realised that he was in a bed. An absurdly comfortable bed at that, and bigger than anything he'd ever slept in. Thomas didn't know what constituted a King size or a Queen size, but he imagined you could probably fit most of the royal family in this bed. You didn't get beds like this in hospital, no matter how private it might be, so that blew that theory out the water.

Rubbing his eyes, he looked round the rest of the room. There was a door to his left, as well as another much larger door in front of him on the other side of the room. The doors looked like they were made of wood and ornately carved, much like the wardrobe and chest of drawers that Thomas could see. Sliding himself out from under the bed sheets, he realised that someone had put him in a set of silk pyjamas. He hadn't worn pyjamas since he was seven years old and he didn't feel like starting again any time soon, so this was the first thing to remedy.

Treading quietly, he crossed over to the wardrobe and opened it. What he saw inside was almost the most surprising thing that had happened to him so far. The wardrobe was full of his clothes. Not just the same brands or type of clothes he usually wore, but his exact clothes from his wardrobe at home. He took out an old blue t-shirt and, sure enough, saw that many of the stitches along one of the hems were loose. His mother was always telling him to get rid of it, but he liked this particular t-shirt. The fact that it was falling apart was irrelevant. The mystery of how all his clothes came to be stored in this strange room spurred Thomas to get changed quickly so as to go find out just what was going on. He changed into the blue t-shirt, seeing as it was already in his hands, as well as a pair of jeans, a grey jacket and his usual trainers (which were sitting at opposite ends of the wardrobe, just like they would have been at home). Fully dressed, he made his way over to the larger of the two doors which led to a wide corridor. He could see more doors lining the other side. The floor looked like marble, which made the sound of approaching footsteps all the more noticeable.

Thomas quickly pulled the door back and held his breath, listening as the footsteps came closer. It sounded like more than one person. As he peered out through the miniscule crack he had left in the doorway, he saw two figures going past the door and continuing on. He hadn't seen enough of them to determine who or, indeed, what they were. For the moment the wisest course of action seemed to be to close the door and think for a moment. He saw the other, smaller door in the corner of his eye. Upon opening it, he found himself looking into an identical room, except the occupant of the bed in this room was still asleep.

'Isaac!' breathed Thomas, quickly stepping into the room and closing the door behind him as quietly as he could. He moved to his brother's bedside and started whispering his name urgently. When it didn't work after a few attempts, he started jostling him. 'Isaac …Isaac! Wake up!'

'No …no, go away,' mumbled Isaac. 'I don't have to get up now, it's the holidays …'

'Will you wake up, you little lump!' growled Thomas, giving his brother an extra vigorous jostle. Isaac finally roused and sat up.

'Tommy! What are you doing in my room? I …I had the worst …'

'Nightmare?' offered Thomas bluntly. 'I had the same, but I'm not so sure it was a nightmare. Also, look around you, Eyes. We're not in your room.'

'Then where are we?' asked Isaac quietly.

'My first thought was hospital …now I'm thinking it's some kind of posh hotel,' said Thomas frankly. 'My room is next door. The wardrobe even has all my clothes in it.' Isaac slowly climbed out of the bed, wearing pyjamas similar to the ones Thomas had found himself in. He crossed over to a wardrobe, took hold of the handle and hesitated for a moment or two before opening it. He glanced back and forth at the garments hanging up inside it. Then he rifled through them and pulled one out at random.

'These definitely aren't my clothes! I mean, look at this!' said Isaac indignantly. He was holding up some bright green dungarees, on the front of which was a sewn on picture of a big, smiley frog. In spite of everything, Thomas couldn't help but snigger. 'Who thinks I'd wear these? That's for little kids!' Isaac dropped the dungarees in disgust and continued rifling through the wardrobe. Every so often he would emit a guttural noise that indicated he'd found something even more hideous than the dungarees.

'Alright, they're definitely not your clothes, but I suggest you find something to put on. We need to get out of here.'

'Why? Couldn't we just stay here?' asked Isaac, taking out the least objectionable shirt he could find.

'Something happened to us, Eyes. I think we may have even been kidnapped.'

'Kidnapped? By who?'

'Don't you remember those guys on the horses? The giant wolf …the bat, and whatever that other monster was?'

'Those weren't in my dream at all …there was Emily reading her stupid book and then …then there was the trees …and then,' Isaac stopped just after changing into the shirt. A vacant yet terrified look came over his face. 'Nothing. There was a terrible …nothing.' Thomas stared intently at his brother. He too remembered those awful few moments where he could literally not feel or think anything. The experience had obviously affected Isaac worse than Thomas or Emily, and Isaac had no memory of their trek through the wasteland or their encounter with the monsters and the mounted fighters. The feeling of nothingness concerned Thomas more than anything else and it was clear that Isaac had felt it too. Thomas quickly explained everything that had happened after their arrival in the wasteland, right up to getting sand thrown at him and losing consciousness.

'And …and you think that all really happened?' asked Isaac slowly.

'It felt too real to have been a dream!' snapped Thomas. 'Besides, how could we both have the same beginning to a dream but not the rest of it? The leader of those men was talking about us 'finding help' and 'being delusional'. That doesn't sound good to me. We have to assume that whatever this place is, they're going to do something to us.'

'Like what?' asked Isaac, now looking very afraid indeed.

'I don't know, but we're not going to wait around to find out. Come on, get dressed quickly. Then we'll go see if we can find Emily.' Isaac looked for a moment as though he wanted to contest that last part, but thought better of it and finished getting changed. As they made their way to the door, they spotted something on top of the chest of drawers.

'My phone!' exclaimed Isaac, picking it up eagerly.

'Your phone? You mean my phone!' growled Thomas as he made a grab for it. Isaac ducked out of his reach but stopped abruptly.

'I don't think it matters whose phone it is. There's no signal at all, no anything!' he moaned, jabbing away at the buttons.

'Just stick it in your pocket and let's get out of here,' Thomas hissed. Isaac slipped the non-functioning phone into the pocket of the dark purple shorts he had found in the wardrobe. There hadn't really been anything in the way of trousers in there, just nauseatingly cute t-shirts and shorts of various colours. It was almost as if whoever picked out the clothes was under the impression that ten-year-olds dressed as though they were still in preschool. Then again, many of the clothes would have been turned down by most self-respecting preschoolers.

The boys carefully opened the door and looked down the corridor. They immediately saw someone coming, but luckily he did not see them. The large pile of books he was carrying made sure of that. They closed the door again.

'Ok, we wait until he's passed the door, then we jump out and get him from behind,' whispered Thomas. Isaac opened his mouth as though to ask a question, but Thomas cut him off. 'We need answers, and we're going to get them.' Thomas pressed his ear to the door, and could definitely hear the heavy footsteps of the man passing the door, made all the more heavy by the weight he was carrying. Waiting only for a few seconds, the two boys pushed open the door and ran in the direction of the passer-by. Thomas jumped onto his back while Isaac, being smaller, went for his legs. The corridor rang with the surprised cry of the man as well as the grunting of the two boys.

Their target quickly lost his balance and sent books tumbling to the floor, followed quickly by his good self and the boys. Not loosening their grip for a second, Thomas, Isaac and the man became a tangled mess of limbs as they struggled on the pristine floor. The man continued to cry out but Thomas soon managed to get his hands round his mouth while Isaac was still making it impossible for the man to stand up. It was not the most masterful of attacks, but it was all they could manage on such short notice. Thomas was about to start demanding answers to a vast number of questions when he heard a familiar voice.

'Oh, will you two stop being so silly?' Struggles ceased and the boys looked up to find their cousin, Emily, standing over them and wearing a smug look (not to mention a rather tasteful summer dress).

'Yes, please do let Clark up. I'm afraid he's not used to such rough-housing,' said another, less familiar voice. Standing just behind Emily was an old man. Grey uncombed hair fell down to his shoulders, which was almost at odds with his neat moustache. His clothes were a motley collection of brown and beige. Before either of the boys could say anything, he offered his hand to help them up. 'Welcome, Thomas and Isaac Llewellyn, to the Library!'

Chapter 5

Of Heroes and Friends

'The …the what?' asked Thomas, still half stuck under Isaac and their unsuspecting victim.

'The Library, I assume you've been in one before? Well, none quite like this one, I'd venture. Come on now, up you get!' The man still had his hand held out, and given their current circumstances, it seemed almost ridiculous not to take it. Soon enough he and Isaac were standing up and the man they attacked had begun to pick up the books he had been carrying. 'My name is Belactacus, and this is my Chief Clerk, Clark. Before you say anything, he's heard all the jokes about his name, most of them from me.' Belactacus smiled at the man scrambling to recover all the books. Feeling guilty over attacking him, Thomas sheepishly picked up some of the books closest to him. He could have sworn he heard Clark mutter something along the lines of 'Thank you'. He was a thin chap who wore spectacles on his pale, unassuming face. Very much the 'indoor and bookish' type, Thomas thought to himself. Isaac merely looked down on Clark, clearly with no intention of helping him.

'What kind of name is 'Belactacus'?' Isaac asked, barely looking up.

'It happens to be my kind of name, seeing as it belongs to me,' said Belactacus lightly, unfazed by Isaac's rudeness. 'I'm certain you have many more sensible questions, but you have been asleep for quite some time and are hungry, no doubt?'

Thomas was hungry, now that this man came to mention it. He'd almost managed to ignore it since he woke up, being altogether too concerned with working out where he was. Seeing the boy's hands come to rest on his belly as a matter of reflex, Belactacus smiled and nodded.

'I thought so. Come with me, please. Clark, Galvina is waiting for those books. Try not to get attacked again on the way, dear boy.' Belactacus turned and began walking down the corridor, Emily close behind him. Thomas handed the books he had picked up over to Clark.

'Sorry for …you know …' he started, but Clark just took the books and mumbled something again, then started off down towards the opposite end of the corridor. Thomas and Isaac quickly caught up with Belactacus and Emily.

'So, just what is this place?' asked Thomas.

'Belactacus told you, it's the Library!' said Emily, who was unable to hide the grin on her face.

'Is that it, just 'a library'?' sneered Isaac.

'Not 'a library', 'the Library', said Emily. 'Don't you listen? This is the ultimate library!'

'I couldn't have put it better myself, young Emily,' said Belactacus, his smile distorting his moustache. 'Though perhaps I should elaborate for the benefit of your cousins. You find yourselves in the Library, a place in which every book known to the human race is stored.'

'That's stupid. You could never build a place big enough to hold that many books …' began Isaac, but stopped abruptly when he nearly ran into Belactacus. The old man had turned to face him, and had bent low so that his own face came within inches of Isaac's. He appeared to scan every last bit of Isaac's face with his eyes, as they were darting backward and forward. He then stopped and stared straight into Isaac's eyes.

'Yes, I thought so. A pity.' Without another word he turned around and carried on walking. Isaac remained rooted to the spot until Thomas jostled him roughly by the shoulder.

'Will you just watch what comes out of your little mouth? He probably has the answers we need!'

'Him? Yeah, right. He's got to be crazy if he thinks one stupid library can hold all those books. A computer with enough memory could store them, yeah …but a …'

'Just …just shut up!' hissed Thomas. Jerking Isaac forward by his sleeve, Thomas made to catch up with Emily and Belactacus again, the two of whom seemed to be engaged in a pleasant conversation. 'Excuse me for interrupting, Belactacus …but you and Emily seem to know each other pretty well considering we only just got here.'

'Ah, well I'm afraid you're only half right there. Your cousin and I have indeed already been talking at great length, on and off, for the best part of two days now, so I'm afraid you have not only just arrived.'

'Two days? We were asleep for two days? No wonder I feel so hungry …'

'Speaking of which, here we are!' said Belactacus as he pushed open a door marked only with a large 'S' ornately carved into it. As soon as the door opened the children could smell something wonderful coming from within. A long table sat in the middle of this room, and along the walls were several ovens, kitchen counters, cupboards and doors that led to larders. The children knew this because out of one of the doors came a short lady carrying armfuls of vegetables. Just as everything about Clark had suggested 'bookish' to Thomas, everything about this woman seemed to suggest 'mother'. Her dark hair was tied back so as not to get in the way of her kindly face. The moment she saw them at the door, she immediately seemed to light up. 'Sylvia, our two other guests are awake.'

'About time too!' exclaimed Sylvia, striding across the room to carefully place the food she had retrieved on the centre table, then advancing on Thomas. Before he could even think of objecting, she had basically grabbed hold of his face but in that gentle way mothers tend to do when they're checking on your general health. 'That Sand might have knocked them out for weeks! Terrible stuff! Well, come on in my lovelies! You must be famished!' Emily went and sat down straightaway, followed gingerly by Thomas and Isaac. Sylvia seemed to be able to move incredibly fast for someone of her stature, because within moments the table was full of bowls and dishes of all kinds of food. Emily began helping herself as soon as the first bowl hit the table, and though cautious at first, Thomas started plating up a meal as well. Sylvia seemed like the type to start fussing if he didn't. Thomas noticed that Emily wasn't eating nearly as much as him or Isaac, but then that made sense if she hadn't been asleep for two days like them.

Belactacus sat at the head of the table with a simple cup of tea. Nobody really said anything until the two boys felt they couldn't eat any more. When Thomas announced this, it was with another flurry of bowls and plates that Sylvia replaced all the food on the table with a vast selection of desserts. Thomas was sensible enough to just take something light, Isaac was not and began tucking in to a large bowl of chocolate ice cream, covered in sprinkles and whipped cream and a bunch of other sweet and sickly things. Belactacus drank the last of his tea and sat back in his chair.

'Now then, Thomas and Isaac …we shall start the onslaught of questions. Emily and I have discussed much of what I have to tell you already, but do feel free, young Emily, to ask any further questions or contribute where you see fit.' He smiled at Emily, who returned the smile as she helped herself to a bowl of sliced fruit. 'So, where shall we begin?'

'How about by telling us where we are?' suggested Thomas.

'Ah yes, a sensible place to start. This may shock you, but you are no longer in your own world. You have, in fact, entered an entirely different realm, a world that exists outside your own universe. You have entered the Realm of Imagination.'

'The Realm of …what?' asked Isaac thickly through a mouthful of ice cream.

'Imagination,' said Belactacus patiently. 'To put it in a nutshell, as you might say, this is the realm where things that are merely imagined in your world come to life.'

'Okay …how about …taking it out of the nutshell for a moment and telling us a little more?' said Thomas, putting down his spoon and giving the old man his full attention.

'Do you recall what happened to you in the wood outside your aunt and uncle's house?' asked Belactacus. The two boys were a little surprised to be asked this. Clearly Emily had told Belactacus a great deal about what had happened to him. They both nodded slowly. 'The wood is important, for what is a wood without trees? Yes, trees are essential. Your race does not know this, but trees contain an element that amplifies the creative thoughts of humans, otherwise known as their imaginations. The element has never been detected by human scientists, and it is unlikely that it will ever be detected. Not only do trees strengthen the thoughts of humans, they also give them form. Have you ever been out walking and thought that something was behind you? An animal or something worse? Perhaps you even saw it in the corner of your eye? That is because, for the most fleeting of split seconds, something was there. You imagined it; it became real and was almost instantly pulled into the Realm of Imagination. You might dismiss it, tell yourself you only saw it in your mind's eye, but you actually imagined it into being. The Realm of Imagination is populated with figments of human imagination, given form and life of their own.'

'So you, Clark and Sylvia …are all imaginary? You're not real?' asked Thomas, who ultimately saw no good reason to doubt what he was being told.

'Not 'real' in the strictest sense, my lovely,' said Sylvia, removing Isaac's empty bowl. 'We're real enough though, I suppose …but we were all imagined by somebody at some point.'

'Ah, but some of us are a little more than just the imaginings of one person, my dear,' said Belactacus.

'True, true. Take me for example. I am the Mother,' said Sylvia, beaming at the children. When Isaac and Thomas said nothing, Emily rolled her eyes and leaned forward.

'She's what thousands of children around our world imagine a mother to be like. You know, children who don't have a mother.'

'Poor dears,' sighed Sylvia. Suddenly, as quick as a flash she had produced a tissue from her pocket and was attempting to wipe the chocolate from around Isaac's mouth. Ignoring his brother's cries of protest, Thomas turned back to Belactacus.

'Can I ask, what's your role here?'

'Certainly you can ask because you're capable of forming the question, just as I am capable of answering. Like Sylvia, I am a manifestation. The collected thoughts of generations focused on one ideal given one form. There are a number of us here in the Realm of Imagination. For my part, over the years humankind has imagined new ways to organise and I am the culmination of the ponderings of those who have sought to bring order to chaotic systems. I owe my very existence to the Dewey Decimal system. In short, I am the Librarian and it is my duty to oversee the Library.'

'It really does contain every book in the world! I've seen it!' exclaimed Emily, unable to contain her excitement.

'Yeah, great …that brings me to another question …well, two really,' said Thomas. 'Firstly, how did we get here when it's apparently only supposed to be imaginary things that come into this realm and just what have you and Emily been talking about while we were asleep?' Belactacus sat back in his chair and frowned. Not at anyone in particular, but it was a deep and troubled frown aimed at the whole situation.

'Sadly, I cannot tell you exactly how you came to be here.'

'Cannot, or will not?' snapped Thomas, who was instantly surprised at his own rudeness and wished he hadn't said it. Belactacus' frown was replaced with a combined look of mild surprise and a stare of stern condemnation.

'I am exceedingly careful with my choice of words, young Thomas. I cannot tell you how you came to be here because I do not know. As you said, only imaginary things are supposed to cross over from your Realm to ours. This is what led the Heroes who found you to believe you were Friends.'

'Hang on … 'Heroes' and 'Friends'? Who are they supposed to be?' asked Isaac with his now thoroughly cleaned mouth.

'The Heroes are fighters, warriors imagined into being by those who most need a protector and find themselves without one. They are, by definition, everyone's idea of a perfect guardian. They were patrolling the borders of the Barren Thought lands when they found you. After they saved you from those Monsters …I assume I don't have to explain what they are?' Thomas felt his whole body stiffen. In a torrent of memories he thought of some of the horrible creatures he had been afraid of when he was little. Large, many eyed monsters in the dark that wanted to eat him. Snake-like creatures that lived under his bed. Upon growing up he had, naturally, convinced himself that these things were not real and could not possibly hurt him. To learn now that such things were real and had come very close to hurting him was an understandable shock.

'Yes,' continued Belactacus softly, 'I can see from your expression that you understand. Monsters are created when a human's own imagination betrays them, or runs away with them as the expression goes. Here, however, they are very real and very dangerous. I believe a wolf was among the Monsters that attacked you? Hardly surprising as wolves feature greatly as vilified predators in so many of your world's cultures. Consider yourselves lucky you didn't come across a dragon.

After you were rescued, Captain Madroc assumed you were imaginary Friends. Companions imagined by children who have no one 'real' to play with. You see, for the most part, Friends enter this realm knowing full well that they are imaginary and settle into their lives here. Now and then, however, some arrive confused and disorientated, unsure of who or what they are. That is what Captain Madroc assumed upon speaking to you.'

'He …he thought we were imaginary?' exclaimed Thomas. 'Well, we're not! We're real! Very real! What can we do to prove it?'

'You don't have to prove anything to me, young Thomas. I am quite convinced that you are, in fact, real children.'

'You are? Uh …how?'

'Luckily for you, your cousin proved to be a little more level-headed than you.'

'It's often the way,' sighed Emily. 'Boys can be so hot headed.' Isaac glared at her, but Thomas didn't take his eyes from Belactacus as he carried on.

'Olath, the Hero who was ordered to bring you here, decided to keep Emily conscious so as to question her during your journey. She wasn't threatening anyone with a deadly rock and did not appear to be ill, so she was spared the Sand. Olath began to suspect that your cousin was not a Friend after all, but a fully real human. He brought you all here to my attention, and I am quite sure I have confirmed his suspicions. You see, Friends usually arrive knowing they are imaginary but with a detailed knowledge of the person who imagined them. Friends who arrive disorientated cannot remember anything about where they came from. For the past two days, Emily and I have been having a series of delightful chats about her good self and her family. More than enough to convince me that she is not a Friend. She has vouched for the two of you as well, but we shall have to convince the Council.'

'Who are they?' asked Thomas, who had gone from being relieved that someone believed he wasn't imaginary to rather apprehensive about having to prove it to some governing body.

'Five representatives, whose duty is to decide what should stay imaginary and what should become real. You see, very occasionally, an animal or a plant may be chosen to return to the Realm of Reality and become real. It is brought before the council and they debate the various pros and cons before voting. The decision must be unanimous, because only the Councillors have the power to open a portal from this Realm to the Realm of Reality. It is the Councillors who need to be convinced that you are real and shouldn't even be here in the first place, not that I haven't found your company to be very enjoyable.' Isaac let out a loud and sudden burp. 'For the most part,' amended Belactacus. While Emily and Thomas laughed and Sylvia admonished Isaac for such a revolting bodily function, there was a knock on the door and Clark entered.

'Excuse me, sir ...but Councillor Torvik has arrived.'

Chapter 6

Meeting the Councillor

'Excellent, thank you Clark!' barked Belactacus, getting up from his seat quicker than one would have thought possible. 'This is the gentlemen I was telling you about, Emily. He holds a great deal of sway on the Council. If we can convince him then I'm sure the meeting with the rest of the council will be a mere formality. Come, we mustn't keep him waiting!'

'Wait a moment!' exclaimed Sylvia before setting about inspecting all three of the children, smoothing down stray strands of hair, straightening collars and removing any remaining traces of food from around their mouths. 'There …there we go my sweeties! You need to look your best for Councillor Torvik. Not that he's one to judge, in fact he's quite lovely! Handsome, too …'

'He's also quite busy, Sylvia. Come now, children!' said Belactacus, motioning towards Clark who was holding the door and looking sheepish. Now that the children looked presentable from top to bottom, Sylvia herded them towards the door. Belactacus and Clark turned right down the corridor and the children followed. After they had been walking for some time, Thomas suddenly noticed the lack of windows. He looked up at the ceiling and saw nothing he recognised as a light source, yet the entire corridor seemed to be flooded with natural light. Light that was just, well, there and not coming from anywhere. He got the distinct feeling that he would see many more things like this, things that made almost no sense whatsoever.

Most of the doors that lined both sides of the corridor looked alike except that a few had odd marks carved into them. Every now and then someone dressed similarly to Clark would emerge from a door, usually carrying books. Every one of them stopped to make some mark of respect when they saw Belactacus coming, who responded in kind each time. Belactacus obviously knew where they were going, though to Thomas the corridor seemed endless. It was Belactacus that slowed down and opened an unmarked door. Emily went in first, in fact she skipped over the threshold. Thomas followed a little more tentatively and Isaac had to be nearly pushed through by Clark, who hadn't forgotten the fact that Isaac still hadn't apologised for his part in tackling him to the ground.

The room in which they now found themselves was certainly the most grand they had seen so far. It looked like a cross between a study and an old fashioned drawing room, the kind of thing Thomas had seen on the television period dramas his mother was so fond of. Shelves of books lined the walls on all sides. Thomas noticed that this room, like the corridor outside, didn't have a single window, yet there was light in abundance. Across from the door was a set of chairs, two of them high backed and winged and one long sofa. Out of one of the two chairs rose a man. He seemed middle aged, though none of the children were quite sure what age exactly that was supposed to mean. He was certainly handsome, even more so when he smiled at the sight of Belactacus and the children. His dark brown hair looked thoroughly combed and well kept. He straightened a dark green tunic as he rose and walked over to shake Belactacus' hand.

'Councillor, thank you for coming,' said Belactacus.

'Not at all, not at all Belactacus!' said Torvik, in a voice that was rich and reassuring. 'These must be the children!' Clark ushered the three of them forward, barely looking up from the intricately patterned carpet. Torvik shook them all by the hand in turn and the children introduced themselves. He

47

motioned for them to sit and they did so on the sofa, while Belactacus and Torvik each took one of the armchairs. Clark stood by the door and looked uncomfortable, something he seemed to be extremely good at. 'Now then, my new young friends,' said Torvik, sitting forward in his chair. 'You should know I have a great deal of respect for Belactacus' judgement. If he says that the three of you are not Friends, I have to say I'm inclined to believe him. On the other hand, you must understand that something like this has never happened before. Humans are not supposed to be pulled from the Realm of Reality, only the things they think of.'

'Well, it happened to us,' sighed Thomas. 'Believe me, it was all very dramatic and I wouldn't want to do it again.'

'I do believe you, Thomas. The process of crossing from one Realm to the other can be a rough experience. That's why Friends sometimes arrive in this Realm confused. It's hardly surprising after they pass through the Void.'

'The what?' piped up Isaac.

'The Void of Nonexistence, young Isaac,' said Belactacus. 'The space, or rather lack of space, that stands between the two Realms. While you travel across the Void, you do not technically exist. You have no thought and no physical being, not until you come out the other side.'

'Do you remember the Void?' asked Torvik gently.

Their short journey through the Void was something all the children had tried very hard to forget. They had known nothing about what was happening to them at the time, as they had no minds in the Void. What Thomas certainly remembered was how suddenly and violently all feeling and sensation had returned to him upon leaving the Void. Just thinking about it, even now, made him tremble. He glanced over at his cousin and brother and saw that they also were visibly shaken.

'Yes, I see you do remember,' said Torvik quietly. 'It's what you remember before you entered the Void that is important. With your permission, I'd like to ask you some questions. May I?' Emily and Thomas nodded silently, while Isaac did nothing at all. 'Emily, what are your parents' names?'

'Kate and Norman Reed,' answered Emily quietly.

'When were you born?'

'August the eighteenth, 2004,' said Emily with a little more strength in her voice. Torvik questioned Emily like this for almost twenty minutes, asking her for stories about her family, her friends and where she came from. The conversation then turned to talk of her future, her hopes and dreams. It turned out she had quite a few. In time he moved on to the two boys, taking an hour overall. Thomas simply answered each question truthfully. Isaac answered almost grudgingly, making the occasional snide remark. No fewer than three of these remarks earned him a nudge in the ribs from Thomas. Early on in Emily's interview, Belactacus had sent Clark to fetch some refreshments. He had returned along with Sylvia, carrying trays of drink and biscuits. Torvik was munching on a chocolate biscuit when Isaac had just about finished telling him about his favourite video game. He held up a finger while he swallowed the last mouthful.

'Thank you, Isaac. I think I've heard enough. The three of you certainly know a great deal about your lives, and why shouldn't you? They're your own lives! The point is Friends who arrive in this Realm confused have no knowledge of a previous existence. Many I've spoken to over the years simply keep insisting they are real, but with time and counselling they come to realise that they were created in the mind of a human child. In this case, however, I am convinced that we have a set of genuine humans in our midst!'

'I'm glad you agree with me, Councillor. The question is what we do with them now they are here?' asked Belactacus.

'Send them home, naturally,' said Torvik, sitting back in his chair. 'That has to be our first priority.'

'Just …how do we go about that?' asked Thomas, sensing that he and his relatives were in danger of being left out of the conversation entirely.

'I shall call for an emergency meeting of the Council. One or two of them might be a little shocked at the prospect of humans in our Realm, but ultimately I think we can persuade them that you are Real and need to be sent home. You see, only all five councillors working together can open a stable portal from this Realm back to the Realm of Reality. Portals coming in to our Realm happen on their own.'

'If that's true, then how did we get here in the first place?' asked Thomas. Torvik winced at this, and for a moment or two didn't seem able or willing to look Thomas in the eye.

'Well, that is something of a mystery. As you've already been told, only imaginary things are supposed to be brought into our Realm. Nothing like this has ever happened before. We will certainly look into it, but that can wait until after we've seen you all safely home. Now, if you'll excuse me, I'll start getting a message out to the other councillors. It's a shame you hadn't arrived sooner in a way. The Council met just a few days ago to send a new species of newt into your Realm. Everybody's left for what counts as a holiday. However, we'll soon have everyone rounded up!'

Torvik rose from his seat and shook the hands of everyone, except Sylvia, to whom he gave an affectionate kiss on the cheek. Clark escorted the children back to their rooms, where they remained all day under the care of Sylvia. Even though they had access to just about anything they wanted to eat and all the care and attention they could ever want from Sylvia, Thomas couldn't help but feel that they were being kept away from something. They were supposed to be in this apparently immense 'Library', yet all he had seen was their bedrooms, the kitchen where they had eaten and the room where they had spoken with Torvik. The only other thing had been the seemingly endless corridor that joined them all together. One thing he had definitely not seen in any of the rooms was a window. No windows, no electric lighting, no candles and yet every room was well lit. This Realm of Imagination that they seemed to have found themselves in did, however, seem to have night and day, because the light in Thomas' room began to dim after a few hours.

Sure enough, Sylvia soon came into all their rooms and insisted that the children get ready for bed. Thomas did indeed get into bed, but his mind was too busy trying to process everything that he had been told, not to mention all that he hadn't been told. He was beginning to think that perhaps, on this one occasion, he might be better off just trusting Belactacus and Torvik. Given the bizarre nature of his situation, he should just wait and see what happens. As his room became dark but with traces of what seemed like moonlight, Thomas found himself sitting on the edge of his bed. Hoping firstly that Sylvia was still awake and secondly that she might have something to help him sleep, he strode across his room to the door, with every intention of trying to find her. Almost as soon as he opened the door he heard footsteps out in the corridor and a pair of now familiar voices. He kept the door open only slightly and pressed his ear to it.

'He's been travelling in the Fanciful Mountains, apparently. Enemy action there ceased some time ago, so he's quite safe. I've every confidence my message will get to him before morning.'

'That accounts for all of them. Expediency is vital here, Councillor.'

'I couldn't agree more.' Torvik and Belactacus strolled down the corridor. Thomas held his breath as they walked past his door. He saw them walk on through the opening he had left. The corridor was partly illuminated as though by moonlight, just like his room. Belactacus was walking on the right hand side, closest to Thomas' door, with Torvik at his left hand side.

'The children must be sent back to the Realm of Reality …before they realise just what they are capable of,' whispered Belactacus. Thomas felt a catch in his throat and nearly made a sound. Perhaps he did, because Thomas could have sworn he saw Torvik turn his head slightly, a smile on his handsome face. Thomas didn't hear the rest of their conversation, but when he was convinced they were far enough away, he closed his door and slumped down to the floor.

Chapter 7

The Library

It was unlikely that Thomas was going to sleep anyway, but after overhearing Torvik and Belactacus, sleep became an impossibility. He lay awake all night, turning over everything he had been told and now everything he wasn't supposed to hear. Just what did Torvik mean by the 'enemy'? Thomas supposed he could have meant those monsters that attacked them, or perhaps some other terrible force in this Realm that nobody had seen fit to tell him about? More importantly, what had Belactacus meant? He seemed determined to get them home, but now it seemed his motivations were not so selfless. Was he afraid of them somehow? Torvik had said that no other human had ever entered the Realm of Imagination. If that was true, then what was it that concerned Belactacus so much? Then again, if it was a lie that must mean other humans had passed through into this Realm before. Thomas couldn't help but wonder what might have happened to them, assuming that there was a 'them' in the first place. One thing was certain; Thomas' previous apathy was long gone. He was now more determined than ever to find out what was really going on.

As his room started to get light again, Thomas sat up in his bed. It was clear that thinking all this over, alone in the night had achieved nothing. He had no way of knowing how long it would take to assemble this Council, but he was not willing to sit around and wait. He was resolved to go looking for answers as soon as the opportunity arose. He had already changed into another set of eerily familiar clothes when there was a knock at the door and Sylvia popped her head in.

'Good morning, sweetie! Breakfast is ready in the dining room.' She disappeared for a moment to retrieve Isaac, while Thomas walked out the door with every intention of going exploring. He stopped in his tracks when he nearly ran into someone.

'Morning, Thomas!' said Emily, altogether too loudly and cheerfully for the time of morning. 'Did you sleep well?'

'Not really, no,' muttered Thomas. From the other room he could hear Sylvia insisting that it was time to get up, the way only a mother can. He could also hear Isaac's protests about the clothes in his wardrobe, having to get up in the first place and just about everything in general. Taking advantage of the commotion, Thomas started to tell Emily what he had overheard. He was about to tell her about what Belactacus had said about them when Emily interrupted.

'Oh, I know who the enemy is. They're the Monsters,' she said casually, 'apparently there are thousands of them in this Realm. Belactacus told me not to worry though, the Heroes keep them at bay. He says they're savage and unorganised. No real threat to the city.'

'What city?' asked Thomas.

'The Impossible City. It's where we are now, or rather the Library is within the city. There's supposed to be lots of other towns and cities, but this is the capital.'

'You said the other day that you'd been to see the Library. Have you seen the rest of the city as well?'

'Well, no. Just the Library.'

'Don't you think it's strange that they're keeping us away from so much? Yes, you've seen the Library but we're being told there's so much more out there and yet we can't see it.

There isn't a single window in this place. How can we trust them when they won't tell us where we really are?'

'You are in the Library in the Impossible City, young man,' said Sylvia sternly as she came out of the room with Isaac in tow. He was wearing a blue and green chequered shirt, bright blue shorts and a sour expression. 'As for trust, you can trust Belactacus, Councillor Torvik and me to know what's best for you right now. Now come along or it'll all get cold!'

Breakfast was far from cold; in fact it was the best Thomas had ever eaten. There had been everything to choose from. Thomas had a full cooked breakfast, Emily had a thoroughly healthy cereal with fruit and Isaac had a small mountain of toast. Sylvia had every possible topping for toast, including some that have never been considered but Isaac, being generally unadventurous, stuck to multiple helpings of his favourite topping. They were almost finished eating when they were joined by Clark. After muttering some general greetings, he sat down at the table and started eating.

'Have you heard anything about the Council?' asked Thomas. Clark had only managed two mouthfuls and appeared annoyed at being questioned during breakfast.

'Nothing yet,' he mumbled. He carried on eating, obviously unwilling to say anything else.

'Listen …I was wondering' said Thomas delicately, ' whether we could get out of here for a bit today and maybe see some of the city?' Clark's spoon stopped halfway to his mouth and he glanced up nervously.

'Afraid not …Belactacus wants you to stay here for now.'

'That's not fair!' exclaimed Isaac. 'Emily's been to see the stupid Library and everything, why not us?'

'The Library is not stupid, Isaac!' said Emily, scandalised. 'Besides, I haven't seen everything. Belactacus took me to the Library because I told him about how much I enjoy reading. I haven't seen the city or anything outside the Library.'

'So how come you get special treatment?' demanded Isaac.

'Well, for one thing, Emily can be trusted not to launch unprovoked attacks on unsuspecting people in corridors,' said Clark. Everyone turned to look at him, and he was obviously unused to the attention as he quickly turned his gaze towards his food. The children didn't know this, but Clark occasionally made attempts at wry humour but was always convinced afterwards that he'd said something silly. At that very moment, someone entered who frequently reinforced his feelings of foolishness; a young, beautiful woman dressed in smart clothes similar to Clark.

'Ah, here you all are! Good morning, Sylvia! I don't suppose you've got the kettle on? I could really do with a coffee.' While Sylvia set about preparing said coffee, the attractive woman held out her hand to Thomas. 'Nice to meet you at last! My name's Galvina. I work with Belactacus and the others here at the Library.'

'N-Nice to meet you too,' said Thomas, who was only half as used to talking to pretty girls as he liked to pretend.

'Has Clark here been yammering your ear off?' joked Galvina, giving Clark a teasing push on the shoulder, then laughing as she pushed back her shoulder length, dark black hair. 'Could talk the hind legs off a Popolopagus, eh Clark?' This time the children couldn't help but laugh a little, mostly because they had no idea what a Popolopagus was. 'He knows I'm only joking, don't you? Anyway, I was actually looking for you guys …oh, thanks Sylvia, you are the best!' Galvina took her cup of coffee from Sylvia and had a sip. 'Needed that …now, what was I saying? Oh yes, we've had word from a few of the Councillors and they're on their way. We should hear from the others fairly soon. It was just bad timing that you guys arrived when so many of them were away.'

'We didn't come here on purpose, you know,' mumbled Isaac grumpily.

'Well, of course you didn't! Now you're here though, you might as well enjoy yourselves! When you've finished, why don't I take you all on a tour?'

'Belactacus said …' Clark started very quietly.

'Oh, he changed his mind,' said Galvina, waving her hand impatiently. 'Just a look around the Library.'

'Yeah, sounds great,' said Isaac, his tone dripping with sarcasm as he fiddled absent mindedly with the remnants of the crust from his toast. Thomas found himself able to say very little, not even to reprimand his brother. He was quite distracted, not only by Galvina's beauty but also by how personable and comfortable she was around everyone. Belactacus was obviously hiding things from them and Clark barely spoke to them, so now at last they were faced with someone who just acted normally around them.

'Oh, believe me, Isaac …you've never seen a Library quite like this!' said Galvina, grinning wickedly as she took another sip of coffee.

That same grin was still there a few minutes later as she led the children down the corridor, with Clark straggling along behind them. 'This is the main corridor of the Library, in fact it's the only corridor in the Library! It goes straight along, and every door leads to a different room,' explained Galvina as they walked. Thomas thought he recognised the door that led to the room they had met Torvik in, but he couldn't be sure. They walked past a few more doors until they came to one all the children knew they would recognise if they had seen it before. For one thing it was a set of double doors, and they were much more intricately carved than any of the others. Galvina grabbed one of the door handles when Clark coughed loudly.

'Um …Galvina …are you sure about this? Belactacus …'

'I already told you, Clark the Clerk, Belactacus said it would be fine for the children to come and look around the Library! He even said it might do one of them some good to crack a book open for the first time in his "short and altogether dull little existence!" Galvina looked very intently at Isaac here, but couldn't keep a straight face. 'Never you mind, Isaac. Personally, I think you're a little sweetheart! Now, come on in guys!' Once again, Emily's enthusiasm was apparent and she nearly knocked the two boys over as Galvina opened the door. Nothing could have prepared Thomas for what he saw. The first thing he noticed was the ceiling, mostly the fact that he could barely see it because it was so high. It was very much like walking into a cathedral, except instead of pews there were bookshelves; immensely tall bookshelves that towered up towards the ceiling. Thomas looked to his left, then to his right and all he could see were row upon row of more bookshelves. Emily was skipping along the aisles, reading the plaques at the end of each bookshelf.

'We've come in via the Fantasy Door! My favourite!' she exclaimed. Before Thomas could even frame the question, Galvina laughed and gestured all around her.

'You see, technically the Library is one unbelievably big room. You could spend days trekking round it and still be in the same section. That's why the corridor outside is smaller than the Library itself, it lets you get from one section to the other a lot quicker.'

'Sounds like something out of an episode of …' began Isaac.

'Yes, I'm sure it does,' interrupted Clark. 'Let's just have a quick look and then …'

'Oh, don't be silly, Clark! Come on, I'll show you how we find a book!' exclaimed Galvina. She took a few steps down one of the aisles and started making a clicking sound with her mouth.

'Does …does the book come to her?' asked Isaac uneasily.

'Don't be ridiculous,' sighed Clark. 'The book is fetched for her.' Isaac was about to ask who fetched the book when the answer flew past his head, causing him to yell. Thomas saw it whizz past, but it wasn't until it came to rest on

Galvina's outstretched arm that he could tell what it was. It looked like a squirrel, only the markings on its fur were more intricate and varied in colour than Thomas, Emily or anyone else had ever seen.

'Flying squirrels have proved to be very effective in retrieving books from high or distant shelves extremely quickly,' explained Clark in a monotone while Galvina was whispering something to the squirrel. It seemed to understand, as it quickly leapt from her arm onto the nearest bookshelf. It climbed up a little way and then leapt again, spreading the flaps between its limbs and gliding over to the opposite bookshelf. It climbed higher again and then glided further away until it was out of sight.

'Just how many books are in here?' asked Thomas.

'All of them. Every book that has ever been published in your world can be found here, in every language,' said Galvina. 'I take it Belactacus told you about how trees amplify the power of imagination in your world? Well, the fact is, trees are made into paper and books are made of paper. Ever since the human race started writing things down and mass producing them, we've had to keep a record here.'

'So wait, you're saying paper works the same way as trees? Thinking of things when there's paper around causes those things to become real and then come here?' asked Thomas.

'Well, yes and no …' began Galvina.

'No, no! That's enough, I must insist!' snapped Clark, surprising everyone. He strode forward until he was mere inches away from Galvina. 'You know as well as I what Belactacus said. Looking around the Library is one thing, but you are …'

'Alright, alright!' exclaimed Galvina, obviously a little taken aback by Clark's sudden outburst. 'I didn't mean anything by it, Clark. Ah, here we are!' The flying squirrel had returned, carrying a book on its back. Galvina seemed grateful for the chance to step away from Clark as she held out her arm for the squirrel to land on. She produced some nuts from her pocket and gave them to the squirrel. As it took them and jumped back onto the bookcase, Galvina walked up to Emily, pointedly ignoring Clark along the way. 'Here you go, Emily, give this one a read. I get the feeling you'll enjoy it!'

Emily thanked her, as all young children should do when given anything, but in particular a book. Thomas took a few steps down one of the aisles, scanning the books as he went. He recognised one or two titles on the spines here and there. He looked further on down the aisle and couldn't see the end of it. His mind nearly boggled at the thought that this was only one section of the Library, housing just one genre. How many other genres could he think of? Science fiction, horror, crime, classics, poems, plays, biographies …though would they count?

'Galvina, what about non fiction books? History, science, biographies? Are they in here?'

'All here, though you'd have to walk across the Library for at least a day to reach that section, or a couple of seconds out in the corridor of course! You see, we need to keep records of non fiction because …'

'That truly is enough this time!' shouted Clark, his voice echoing in the naturally quiet Library. 'Out, the three of you out and back to your rooms!' With nothing from Galvina but an apologetic look, the children were shepherded out of the Library by Clark, who continued to mutter angrily to himself all the way down the corridor. As he was shown back to his room, Thomas couldn't help but feel that even though he had been shown this Library that everyone around here seemed so proud of, there was still a great deal more that was being kept from him.

Thomas waited for an hour or so in his room, then made the decision that if he wanted answers, he would have to go looking for them himself. Going out to explore the corridor had to be better than sitting around doing nothing. He even flattered himself that he might find a way out and then be able to come back for Emily and Isaac. Having listened at his bedroom door and heard nothing outside, he opened the door quietly and slipped out into the corridor. He decided to avoid the direction he had been led down so far and headed the other way. As luck would have it, the corridor was entirely deserted as he went from door to door, looking at the markings on each of them. Not a single one made any sense to him, though some seemed more ornate than the others, similar to the doors they went through to enter the Library itself. He remembered what Galvina said about certain doors leading to specific sections of the Library. What he was most interested in right now was an exit. A library had to have an exit, it stood to reason, but he had been walking for some time now and there didn't seem to be an end to the corridor in sight. Out of frustration more than anything else, he picked a door at random and opened it.

At first he thought he had entered the Library again, but soon came to realise this room was much too small. What made him think of the Library were the many books lining the walls of the room. It looked as though every inch of wall space was taken up by a bookshelf. There was a comfortable looking, high backed armchair towards the end of the room. A little table stood next to it and you will not be surprised to hear that a pile of books sat upon it. In the middle of the room was a large desk, but you may be surprised to hear that not a single book could be seen on it. As Thomas moved further into the room, he could see a great many papers arranged in neat piles on the desk, but another item immediately caught his eye. On the end of the desk was a globe. Thomas immediately recognised it as Earth, but this was not a plastic globe with the countries all in different colours. This one looked remarkably real, as though a miniature version of Earth were sat right there on the desk. The oceans looked like they would be wet to the touch, and indeed Thomas felt a sudden urge to touch the globe itself, specifically to plunge his fingers right into the Atlantic ocean.

'I'll thank you not to touch that,' said a voice behind him. Thomas knew it was impossible to literally jump out of your skin, but he came close enough. He turned on the spot and saw that Belactacus was standing by the door, a book in his hand. Thomas edged away from the globe and let his hand fall to his side. Belactacus crossed the room and placed it on one of the shelves. 'Do you read, Thomas?' he asked without looking at Thomas.

'I ...well, yes ...every now and then.'

'And just what does that mean, "every now and then"?' asked Belactacus, 'when the Internet is down, when the television is broken or when your teacher requires you to?'

Thomas had expected to be thoroughly told off, perhaps even thrown from the room. This current line of questioning threw him completely. He was trying his best not to let it show.

'You seem to know a lot about our world,' he said icily.

'Mostly from reading, and certain other means,' said Belactacus, his eyes darting momentarily to the globe on the desk. It was not missed by Thomas, though he kept his own eyes firmly on the old man. 'Written communication truly is the greatest invention of the human race,' continued Belactacus, now walking along the wall. He ran his fingers over the spines of several books as he walked. 'These books here are just some of my all-time favourites. The right collection of words bound to sheaves of paper can inspire millions ...or devastate an entire world.' His voice trailed off and then suddenly his hand leapt forward and retrieved a book from the shelf to his left. He carried the book quite nonchalantly to his desk, behind which he sat. 'I understand you paid a visit to the Library earlier today?'

'Yes,' said Thomas curtly. 'Very impressive.'

'I'm glad you approve,' said Belactacus, 'I also understand you were asking certain questions.'

'Any chance of certain answers?' asked Thomas abruptly.

'That depends entirely on the questions,' said Belactacus, who was now smiling as though thoroughly enjoying himself.

'How about this one, then? I get that books are made from paper, and that like the trees they came from it gives your imagination a boost …so does that mean that every time someone reads a book, they're creating all the characters and things here?'

'Not exactly, no. Not while they're reading the book, anyway. After all, no two people interpret a character in a book exactly the same way, now do they?'

'So why exactly do you have a copy of every book ever made here?' Thomas went on.

'To anchor each and every one of them,' answered Belactacus. This time Thomas couldn't hide his confusion. Belactacus' smile only got wider. 'You see, as long as we have a copy of that book somewhere here, in the Library, the characters and scenarios contained therein remain in the mind of the reader. Otherwise we'd have many thousands of consulting detectives cluttering up the place, not to mention goodness knows how many flying boys or talking scarecrows. Without this Library, indeed without this Realm, the chaos would be …well, unimaginable, if you'll pardon the expression.'

'What about non-fiction books? I asked about them and Clark went off on one …'

'Yes, I know,' said Belactacus, suddenly a tad more stern, 'I think you have learned quite enough for now. Good day.' Belactacus turned his attention to the book he had retrieved and Thomas, quite naturally, assumed he had been dismissed. Just as he reached the door handle, however, he heard Belactacus speak again. 'I think perhaps, for the time being, you would be well advised to stay in your room, Thomas. In fact, I insist upon it.'

'I …but I …'

'Thought that you could enter someone's private study without permission and escape some form of punishment?' Belactacus offered, 'Perhaps you have a better imagination than I gave you credit for. Nevertheless, apart from mealtimes, you shall remain in your room until we hear from the Council. Good day.' Thomas made to protest, but the only words he could think of were "That's so unfair!", and they sounded like an unbearable cliché for someone his age. Being aware of that, he simply closed the door behind him and went back to his room.

Chapter 8

Journey to the Tower of Realms

Another whole day passed with no news. Emily was allowed to make escorted visits to the Library for more books, but Isaac couldn't be persuaded to join her. He tried to use Thomas' phone to play games but the battery soon ran out, leaving him with no other pastime but complaining. Thomas, on the other hand, spent every available minute going over what he already knew, trying to see if there was something anyone had said that he hadn't really taken on board at the time. The only person he saw now was Sylvia for mealtimes and she steadfastly refused to answer any of his questions, though she shared the children's dissatisfaction at them being cooped up. In her opinion, little boys and girls should be able to go out to play, but Belactacus' instructions had been very clear. By the second day since he had woken up to find himself in the Library, there was finally some news. Clark came when they had just finished breakfast to bring them to the same meeting room they had met Torvik. This time Belactacus was there with a strange man. Just how strange will soon become clear.

'Ah, come on in!' said Belactacus. 'Children, this is Hervium. He's going to serve as your advocate before the Council.' Hervium was a good deal shorter than Belactacus, in fact he wasn't much taller than Isaac. He wore thick glasses and was balding. He was wearing smart clothes, which was all anyone seemed to wear round here, but he was also wearing a set of green robes over his suit. He tucked a large folder full of papers under one arm and offered his other hand to each of the children in turn.

'A pleasure, simply a pleasure to meet you all! Now, the good news is all the Councillors have arrived in the city and the, well even better news is that they'll be seeing you this morning. This really is an emergency session, given the circumstances.'

'If it's such an emergency, how come we've been cooped up here all this time?' demanded Isaac. 'I've been so bored!'

'B-Bored? In the Library?' asked Hervium, looking utterly shocked at the very idea. 'Well …well I'm sorry if that's been the case, young man, but not to worry. Soon you'll be back in your own Realm with your family.'

It was then that a sudden and dreadful feeling came over Thomas. A realisation that felt like a hard punch to the stomach, with another punch to the head for good measure. He had been so busy trying to find out what was going on that he hadn't given much thought to his parents or his aunt and uncle. They must be worried sick and had probably called the police. When Thomas voiced these concerns, Hervium merely smiled.

'Ah, not to worry about that, young …young …Thomas,' he said as he checked a sheet of paper in the folder he was carrying. 'From what we know, it's almost certain that once you left your Realm and came into ours, your family almost completely forgot that you exist.'

'They do almost remember you,' interjected Belactacus, sensing that Hervium's lack of tact was going to upset someone. 'They'll remember you as something they might have once dreamed of. When you return, so will their memories.'

'How do we explain where we've been all this time?' asked Emily.

'A good question uh …Emily! That's where the Explanology Department comes in. We have a team that will devise a very good reason for your absence and then our Explanologists will plant those same reasons in the minds of your parents. It's a complicated process and I don't pretend to fully understand how it's all done, but I'm given to understand it's quite painless. We do the same to explorers and scientists in your world who come to be convinced they've discovered a new species of animal or plant. The truth is, of course that someone imagined the new species and we …that is to say, the Council, decided to return it to the Realm of Reality. Sometimes the explanations aren't always believed straightaway …that whole platypus incident, for example …but it all works out in the end! Now, before we go …I'd just like to clarify one or two little things …'

Hervium and the children spent the next two hours going over everything they had told Belactacus and Torvik since their arrival. Isaac began to lose patience after the first twenty minutes, but Hervium insisted that he needed to be sure of the facts before their meeting with the Council. Finally, when all was said and done, they all made their way out of the meeting chamber and down the corridor. Along the way, they were ambushed by Sylvia, who could hardly allow them to appear before the Council without making sure they were looking their best. Once she was done with them and had said her goodbyes, the children were led down the corridor by Belactacus, Clark and Hervium, who was still wearing a contented smile on his face. As they walked, Galvina came out of one of the doors. She could only smile and give them a thumbs up as they passed, much to the obvious displeasure of Clark. Thomas wanted to ask why Galvina wasn't coming with them, but decided against it. He soon realised that he could now actually see the end of the corridor and a door. Clark reached it first and opened it. Thomas got the distinct impression that they were about to leave the Library.

Impressions, when distinct, are often correct. They did indeed step outside onto a paved courtyard. Sunlight and a gentle breeze felt marvellous after so much time indoors.

Belactacus, Clark and Hervium did not slacken their pace, so the children had to take it all in as they walked. The courtyard led to a set of stone steps, which in turn led to a street, but not like any street any of them had ever seen. People of literally all shapes and sizes were coming and going, not just along the street but into the courtyard towards the Library as well. Some looked relatively human, whereas some had ridiculously long noses or enormous ears. Some were bright green, or purple, or any one of a number of colours. Some didn't look human at all, more like blobs of goo that crawled along or great hairy creatures that walked along peaceably.

The buildings along the other side of the street all looked different. Some even looked like they shouldn't be physically possible. Some were upside down with a door at the top of the house but with no obvious means of getting up there. Some were wallpapered on the outside. One looked like it was made out of plastic building blocks. Some leaned forwards, right out into the street, as though they were on the verge of collapse. Noises of all kinds filled the air as the children and their escorts descended the steps. Hervium led them to their left, where they saw a set of steps leading up to a solitary platform. A sign above the steps read 'OverGround Railway: The Library'. The second that Hervium set foot on the first step, the rest of the steps began to move upwards like an escalator. The children followed him, this being the least surprising thing they had seen yet, followed closely by Belactacus and Clark. When they reached the platform, Thomas looked all around but could not see any kind of track.

The platform was empty but for a few people standing by, all wearing the same blue uniform with bright, shining buttons. Nothing else about them seemed the same. A guard standing nearest to Emily had purple tentacles sticking out of his tunic sleeves, yet his face was cat-like. They had only been standing on the platform for a few moments when Hervium looked to the left, then produced a watch from his pocket.

'It's on time today. That makes a most pleasant change!' he chuckled to no one in particular. Thomas and Isaac were about to ask what Emily had already worked out. Before any of them could say another word, there came a loud whistle from somewhere nearby. Slowly, a train track began to materialise in the air in front of the platform. The children looked to their left and saw that a large, green steam train was flying towards them. Well, not flying exactly, as it behaved the way any ordinary train would pulling into a station. The only exception here was the train was many feet off the ground with no visible means of support and the track only seemed to materialise in front of it as required. The train was pulling three coaches, and it was into the first coach that the three children were hurried into once the train had stopped. Clark was the last to get on, and just as he closed the door behind him, the cat-faced guard raised a tentacle and blew into a whistle. The train slowly pulled away as more track appeared in front of it.

The coach was an old fashioned one comprising two long seats on either side. The children were seated in the middle, with Belactacus on one side of them and Clark on the other. Hervium sat on the opposite seat, taking out his folder again and perusing it. It suddenly struck Thomas that Belactacus and Clark may have chosen their seats deliberately so as to stop him, Isaac or Emily getting too good a look out of the window. Indeed, when he made a bit of a show of craning his neck to get said look, Clark's expression soured more than usual and he pulled a blind down.

'There isn't a great deal to see, I'm afraid,' said Belactacus lightly. 'Besides, it won't be long until we arrive.' Thomas couldn't help but feel that there was a lot to see. His brief glimpse told him that much of the city consisted of more weird and wonderful buildings like the ones they had seen outside the Library. There was no way of telling just how big the city was, but Thomas was willing to bet it was vast. He was only half listening to Belactacus, who was reminding them how to behave during the meeting with the Council. He stressed how important it was to let Hervium do the talking and to only speak when spoken to. They would have a chance to answer questions put to them by the Council and they must do so respectfully and truthfully. Clark did a great deal of nodding and made general noises of approval. Belactacus had just about finished his lecture when the train began to slow down. Upon it stopping, they stepped out onto a platform similar to the one they had just left, except the sign above this one read 'Tower of Realms'. They descended another set of moving steps to find themselves facing the tallest tower any of them had ever seen. Indeed it was the tallest tower any human had ever seen, for the Tower of Realms stands several storeys above anything built in the human world. The tower was made from flawless blue stone, with a number of large, domed buildings at its base, all surrounded by a large grey wall. The structure of the tower itself reminded Thomas of a set of child's building blocks, for here and there the tower jutted out slightly. It was towards a large, open gateway in the wall surrounding the tower that they made their way.

Hervium led the way across a large courtyard that joined up many of the buildings at the base of the tower. Everywhere there were people coming and going, but just like at the Library they made way for Belactacus. They walked straight across the courtyard and entered through a large door at the very base of the tower, where Hervium led them across a large reception room, through a door and into a waiting room.

'Take a seat, yes …make yourselves quite comfortable. Now it shouldn't be long before we're called through. I'll just nip through and let them know you're all here, safe and sound …yes …' With that, Hervium disappeared back through the door to the reception. Isaac and Emily both sat down, but one looked entirely at ease while the other seemed uncomfortable in every possible way. Thomas found that he was too restless to sit, and he almost found himself resenting Belactacus as he took a seat.

'Belactacus, what happens if the Council doesn't believe us?' Thomas asked.

'I wouldn't worry about it, Thomas. I shall be testifying, and we know Councillor Torvik believes that the three of you are real. The decision of the Council to return anything to the

Realm of Reality has to be unanimous, but ultimately I see no reason why the other Councillors should vote against you. Trust me, this is merely a formality. Once the Council decide to send you back, all that remains is to place an Explanation in the minds of your parents, and you'll be sent home. All very straightforward.' As they waited for a few more minutes, Thomas still found it hard to settle. He remained standing until the door reopened and Hervium appeared, gesturing for them all to follow him. As Thomas reached the door, he felt a hand on his shoulder followed by a gentle squeeze. It was Belactacus in what he assumed was intended to be a comforting gesture. Thomas forced a smile onto his face and fought the urge to force the hand from his shoulder. Luckily Belactacus released him before he lost his composure and they all made their way out across the reception. They crossed it and came to a large staircase. It split into two directions and they were led to the right. A short walk down a corridor brought them to a double door which opened for them.

The Council Chamber was smaller than Thomas had expected, the only sizeable space being a large circle at the centre of the room. On the side of the circle closest to the door was a series of chairs, in front of which sat two wooden desks. On the opposite side was an elevated, curved desk. Thomas assumed that was where the Council members would be seated. Hervium guided them all to the left hand desk, seating the children at the desk itself while Clark and Belactacus took two of the chairs behind them. The door behind them opened again, and a man entered carrying a folder roughly the same size as Hervium's. He wore robes similar to Hervium's except his were dark blue. He was followed closely by two other people, a tall, pale man and a short, round faced woman. The three of them made their way to the unoccupied desk, not one of them making any kind of move to acknowledge the presence of the children or the others.

'I had no idea that Jarvix had been selected,' whispered Belactacus to Hervium, leaning forward in his seat.

'Well, someone had to be. Protocol and all that,' sighed Torvium.

'Even so, he's not going to hold back. He obviously …'

'What is he here for exactly?' asked Thomas. A fleeting look of annoyance came across Hervium's face as he turned away from Belactacus to face Thomas, who had dared to interrupt their conversation.

'He's here to argue against your being sent back to the Realm of Reality.'

'What?' hissed Thomas, who could practically feel Isaac shaking in the seat next to him. Even Emily let out a tiny squeak of shock. 'You never said someone would be arguing against us! What else haven't you told …' Thomas' whispered rant was cut short when a booming voice rang throughout the room.

'All rise for the honourable Councillors!'

Chapter 9

The Council

A door at the back of the chamber opened. A man dressed in maroon robes entered. The robes were ornately decorated with gold trim around the shoulders, with silver patterns stitched into the sleeves. The man reminded Thomas of the Heroes who had saved him and the others back in the wasteland. He had a strong bearing, tall and muscular, yet he seemed older than the Heroes Thomas had met. This man was closely followed by a ...well, to be perfectly honest it looked like a dog that had been trained to walk upright. It was also wearing maroon robes, as was the woman who came in next. She looked entirely human, with grey hair tied back tightly in a bun. Her face looked as though it had spent many years set in a stern expression, unlike Torvik who walked in behind her, looking even more dashing than he had a few days ago. He gave the children a warm smile as he ascended the steps that led to the elevated desk at which the rest of his colleagues were now sitting.

The last Councillor to come in would have been more surprising to the children had they not seen others like it on their way from the Library. Being mostly a blob, it looked as though it had been poured into the robes and then left to set like jelly. Its light green skin pulsated as it travelled, for as it had no legs it couldn't exactly walk. The blob did move surprisingly fast though as it slithered up the steps to take a seat next to Torvik. Seated together, they certainly made for a strange yet impressive group.

The stern-looking woman, sat in the middle of the others, was the first to speak.

'This emergency meeting of the Council of Reality is hereby called to order. Councillor Milanda chairing, Councillors Callion, Clou, Torvik and Gumm are all present. Advocates, step forward.' Hervium and Jarvix got up from their respective desks and stepped out into the open space in front of the Council, each keeping to their own side. 'Advocate Hervium, present your opening statement,' commanded Councillor Milanda. Hervium gave a very professional-looking bow.

'Madam Chair, the case I bring before you today has warranted the utmost secrecy from the very beginning. We may not have believed it possible, but nevertheless, it has happened. I have here, sitting at this very desk, three human children.' At this, Hervium gestured dramatically towards Thomas, Isaac and Emily. Thomas couldn't help but feel that Hervium's speech seemed a little over-rehearsed. He hadn't been nearly this eloquent when talking to them so far. He also couldn't help but feel frustrated at having to let someone else do all this talking for them. Someone they'd only just met and couldn't remember their names as well. Thomas was often in the habit of not being able to help how he was feeling, but the same can be said for most fourteen-year-olds. Thomas snapped himself away from his own thoughts when he realised that Hervium was still talking.

' …which ultimately means that we humbly and with all due respect to your august persons request that the Council return these children to the Realm of Reality with great expediency.'

'Madam Chair, this is all beyond ridiculous!' exclaimed Jarvix, jumping up from his seat.

'Advocate Jarvix, you have not yet been recognised by this Council,' said Councillor Milanda evenly.

'I apologise, Madam Chair but what Advocate Hervium is suggesting is preposterous! Never before in the history of our Realm has a human crossed the void. They cannot even see or be affected by the portals in any way! It has long been established that only figments of human imagination can enter our Realm. It's a sheer impossibility for a human to do the same!' The children had to stop themselves from laughing, for all through this tirade, Jarvix had been waving his arms about in grand, indignant gestures.

'I have to say I agree with Advocate Jarvix,' said a deep, rumbling voice that came from the blob-like Councillor. 'A human has never entered our Realm before, so why should we believe it has happened now?'

'Councillor Gumm, I understand your ...uh, scepticism ...but we have a number of people ready to testify that they are more than convinced that these three ...children are real,' said Hervium, a little shaken by the sudden turn of events.

'I'm sure you have, but I'd be highly surprised if you had any solid evidence, for there can be none,' sneered Jarvix.

'That's quite enough, Advocate Jarvix,' said Councillor Milanda, rather loudly and clearly. 'Advocate Hervium, this is indeed a most unusual case and I'll admit that I too am sceptical about the possibility of humans in our Realm. However, we shall begin by hearing from the children themselves.' Hervium looked flustered as he turned from the Councillors to the children. His eyes darted between them, obviously trying to decide who to send up first. In the end he chose Emily, making urgent gestures for her to come with him. As she got up, a chair rose from the floor in the middle of the circle and Emily sat down on it. She was a picture of composure. Councillor Milanda leaned forward, her face softening a little. 'What is your name, young lady?'

'Emily Reed, Madam Chair,' said Emily politely. Councillor Milanda proceeded to ask Emily many of the same questions that Belactacus, Torvik and Hervium had already asked. Almost everyone in the room was hanging on Emily's every word. The Councillors, Jarvix and his aides, Belactacus,

Hervium and Clark were all listening intently, but to Thomas and Isaac it was old news. Though in all fairness, they were learning more about their cousin than they ever thought they'd know in their lifetimes. After Milanda had asked most of the usual questions, she asked one that surprised everyone.

'Now Emily, I want you to think hard now. What do you remember of the child who Imagined you?'

'I …I'm sorry, Madam Chair, but nobody "Imagined" me at all. I'm a real person,' said Emily a little uncertainly.

'Please know that no one here will be angry. You are not in trouble. You can tell us the truth,' Milanda pressed.

'I am telling the truth!' said Emily, more hotly than usual; she was not used to having her word doubted.

'I see. Very well, Miss Reed, you are excused,' said Milanda, giving nothing away in the tone of her voice. Emily climbed down from her chair, looking unsettled for the first time since arriving in the Realm of Imagination. She looked at Belactacus, but he was staring resolutely at Councillor Milanda, who met his gaze and matched it, stare for stare.

'The Chair recognises Librarian Belactacus,' said Councillor Milanda, not breaking eye contact with him for a moment. Belactacus gave a curt bow to the Council as a whole before sitting in the seat Emily had just vacated, though the chair itself suddenly became slightly bigger in order to accommodate his adult frame. 'Belactacus, how did these children come to your attention?'

'They were brought to me by Olath, a Hero patrolling the Barren Thought lands. He and Emily had discussed much on their journey to the city and he became convinced that she and her cousins were not Friends.'

'Councillor Callion, is this Olath known to you?' asked Councillor Milanda, turning to the large gentleman who had first entered.

'I believe he serves under Captain Madroc,' said Callion, his tone even and steady.

'Tell me, he is known to be an expert in matters of Reality and Figments?' asked Milanda scathingly.

'Most likely not, but I am, Madam Chair,' said Belactacus loudly. Councillor Milanda's face spun round to face him again, resuming the hard glare she had held before. 'Olath brought them to me so that I might question them as well. Having done so, I in turn contacted Councillor Torvik and requested this emergency meeting. I assure you, Madam Chair, these children are Real and must be returned to the Realm of Reality immediately.'

'Madam Chair, may I be allowed to speak?' asked Jarvix, exercising a little more restraint than before but still giving his arms plenty of exercise. Milanda merely gestured for him to proceed and he strode forward so as to face Belactacus in his seat. 'Belactacus, do you realise not only the absurdity but the impact of what you are saying? If what you are saying were indeed true, it would mean …'

'I am fully aware of what the presence of humans in our Realm means, Advocate Jarvix. That is precisely why I sought to bring this matter to the attention of the Council so urgently.'

'Wait, what do you mean by ...' began Thomas, leaning forward in his seat but he was interrupted by Councillor Milanda snapping her fingers. The resulting sound was unusually loud and echoed throughout the chamber.

'The Chair does not recognise you at this time. Advocate Hervium, kindly keep your client in check.'

'Our most humble apologies, Madam Chair', said Hervium. He was trembling now. Obviously this was not going as he had hoped. He quickly turned to Thomas and stared at him imploringly, making small but frantic hushing gestures. Councillor Milanda turned her attention back to Belactacus.

'Belactacus, with all due respect, it seems infinitely more likely that these children are Friends who have arrived here in our Realm confused and disorientated.'

'Madam Chair, with equally due respect, Friends who arrive disorientated have no knowledge of a previous life. Thomas, Isaac and Emily all have detailed memories of their lives in the Realm of Reality.'

'Even so, it has still not been explained how they arrived in our Realm if they are indeed real,' said Milanda. 'It is supposed to be impossible.'

'I cannot explain how they arrived, but our wisest course of action would be to return them now and then begin an investigation, so as to stop it from happening again.'

'I have heard enough,' snapped Milanda. 'You do not have the authority to advise the Council to do anything, Belactacus. You also forget that the Council has sole control over the portals between the two Realms.'

'You control outgoing portals, Madam Chair, not incoming ones. The children were in a forest when the portal appeared. Incoming portals are always strongest close to trees, perhaps on this occasion the portal was too strong …'

'And pulled three human children in?' said Clou, the dog-like Councillor. 'I'm sorry, Belactacus, but the portals have never even been perceived by humans before. I agree with Councillor Milanda, these children are clearly Friends. They obviously need help adjusting to life in this Realm and should have been brought straight to the CFI. You do them wrong by indulging them.'

'Unless it is not indulgence …perhaps you really do believe them?' suggested Milanda slyly.

'I stand by my own reason and judgement, honourable Councillors. I am, however, not the only one here who believes them.'

At this, Belactacus turned his gaze to Torvik, who had so far remained silent. He sat forward in his chair, his hands clasped together.

'I do believe …that the possibility of humans in our realm needs to be seriously considered. We all know the ramifications. Though perhaps I was hasty …'

'I should say so, Councillor Torvik,' snapped Milanda. 'If even so much as a rumour of this got out, it could cause mass panic.' Thomas had to use all his self-restraint not to speak out again. It was clear nobody was going to explain why their presence was so dangerous, so it seemed pointless to ask. Isaac, apparently, did not agree.

'Why? Are you lot afraid of us or something?' he exclaimed, causing Milanda to snap her fingers again.

'Silence! Advocates, you will hand over all documentation and the Council will retire to deliberate.' Casting a nervous look at Thomas, Hervium gathered up his file and then turned to hand it all over to Milanda. Jarvix had done the same, only he looked a great deal calmer. Having collected all their files, Milanda handed them to Torvik and rose, followed by the rest of the Council. They left the chamber through the same door they had entered. The second it had closed behind Councillor Callion, Thomas rounded on Hervium.

'Ok, I get that you won't tell us why everyone's making such a fuss about us being here, but it's time for a few straight answers! That didn't go as planned, did it?'

'Well …no, Terence …not quite,' said Hervium.

'I've never known Councillor Milanda to be so set against anything,' said Belactacus, who had left the chair and come to join them at the desk. The chair in the centre of the circle had melted back into the floor without a trace.

'I agree, Belactacus …she's normally more willing to listen …'

'Councillor Milanda knows when she's listening to drivel, Hervium,' said Jarvix, who had come over from his own desk. 'Everyone knows humans can't enter our Realm, that's how it is meant to be. I haven't had a chance to introduce myself properly, children …'

'Now see here! You have no right to address my clients, Jarvix!' said Hervium, regaining some composure.

'Somebody needs to tell them how things really are. Quite frankly, I'm surprised at you both. These poor, confused Friends need guidance and help.'

'If they were indeed Friends, they would have it. We're not all so unnerved by the prospect of humans in our Realm that we deny it outright,' said Belactacus, moving to stand between Jarvix and the children. Jarvix looked up into Belactacus' face, back at the children, then sighed and shook his head before returning to his own desk.

Once again Thomas felt the need to ask why humans in the Realm of Imagination was getting everyone so flustered, but instead decided to focus on the possibility of getting home. To that end, he enquired how long the Council would take to decide. Neither Belactacus nor Hervium could be sure, but they had a feeling they wouldn't be long. As it turned out they were right. Only half an hour had passed when the door at the back of the chamber opened and the Councillors re-entered, taking their seats once more.

'The Council has made a decision,' said Milanda. 'In a unanimous vote, we find that the children known as Thomas, Isaac and Emily are not eligible for entry to the Realm of Reality. Furthermore, given their disorientated condition and advanced state of delusion, they will be immediately referred to the CFI to receive care and support. This session is concluded.' Without another word, the Councillors all stood and left. It was then that the man and woman who had come in with Jarvix approached the children.

'If you'll come with us, please. We're here to help you,' said the woman. 'My name is …'

'I don't give a damn what your name is!' shouted Thomas, knocking his chair over as he rapidly rose and backed away. 'We're not imaginary! We don't need your …'

'Now, young man …perhaps for the m-moment …it would be best …' said Hervium quietly.

'No! You've been no help at all! You can all go …'

'Thomas!' shouted Emily, so loudly that it startled all around her. 'Getting angry now isn't going to help us. I trust Belactacus, and he's not going to just abandon us.'

'Indeed not, Emily,' said Belactacus. 'I have every intention of getting to the bottom of all this, and we can appeal the decision of the Council.'

'What good will that do? You heard them!' exclaimed Isaac. 'They've already made up their stupid minds about it!'

'Shut up, Eyes …' said Thomas wearily. As much as he hated to admit it, Emily was right. For the moment they needed to trust Belactacus and Hervium. He, Emily and even Isaac agreed to go with the man and woman peacefully. As they left the chamber, Thomas looked back at Belactacus, Clark and Hervium all deep in discussion. Thomas couldn't help but think back to that moment in the wastelands when those monsters were bearing down on them. Somehow, he felt more helpless now than he had then.

Chapter 10

Looking For a Friend

As they walked out of the Tower of Realms, back across the courtyard and out onto the street, Thomas could only think of one benefit to this whole situation. At least now nobody was trying to hide the rest of the city from their eyes. On the contrary, their escorts suggested walking so that the children could 'get a feel for their new home'. The man and the woman had introduced themselves, but Thomas was past caring about names. He was too busy considering how long to give Belactacus and Hervium to sort all this out before taking matters into his own hands. He didn't intend to exercise patience for long. It was a satisfying notion, the idea of breaking away from those who wanted to keep him here, turning down the aid of those who wanted him gone and getting his cousin and brother home all by himself. Thinking about it helped to quell the sense of frustration that pounded through his very being. The only problem was he had no idea how he was going to do it. A setback, most certainly.

As it turned out the walk to the CFI wasn't altogether that long and naturally the children noticed more weird and wonderful buildings and people along the way. It was soon explained to them that CFI stood for 'Centre for Friend Integration', and it was by far the most clinical place they had come across. Not only that, but it was by far the most boring building they'd seen in the city. It was altogether plainer on the outside than all the strange and colourful buildings around it. A tiny little reception led on to several little consulting rooms and offices. They were taken upstairs and shown to their own rooms as well as a communal room and kitchen. There were plenty of consoling things being said in pleasant tones but Thomas took very little notice. Two things that did sink in, however, were that they would be having their first counselling session in the morning and while they were free to use the communal room, they would not be allowed out of the CFI unsupervised. Not until they'd been deemed 'ready to integrate'. The whole point of this place was to help imaginary friends who couldn't bring themselves to believe they were figments of someone else's imagination. Indeed, they were introduced to several Friends in the communal room, all coming to terms with what they were. While Emily never forgot her manners and spoke to them all, Thomas and Isaac kept to themselves until that evening, when the time came for them all to retire to their own rooms.

Hours later, despite his frustrations, Thomas had managed to fall asleep. Unfortunately it was far from a peaceful, contented sleep. He was dreaming about being back at his aunt and uncle's house. He recognised the garden and saw the same door his mother had stepped out of to tell him to go and find Emily. Elated, he sprinted across the garden and into the house. His mother and father were inside, but they didn't recognise him. They became angry and ordered him out of the house and in spite of all his pleas to the contrary, they claimed never to have seen him before in their lives. He had just been thrust out of the house when he was awoken, rather suddenly, by a hand over his mouth. Naturally he did what anyone would do in this situation which is try to cry out even though there's little point. He could see that someone was standing over him. Whoever it was raised a finger to their lips, then reached over and turned on the bedside lamp. Once his eyes had adjusted to the sudden bright light, Thomas saw that it was Galvina, who retracted her hand from his mouth.

'Galvina? What …'

'No time to explain right now. Get dressed while I get Emily and Isaac. Hurry!' she whispered urgently. Galvina quickly slipped out of the door that led to the other rooms, leaving Thomas to dress. Unlike back at the Library, the wardrobe in Thomas' room here was not full of his clothes from home, but he just about managed to dress himself presentably anyway. Moments later, the door opened again and Galvina appeared, beckoning him out of the room. As he entered the dim corridor he could just make out Isaac and Emily, both fully dressed. After closing the door to Thomas' room, Galvina gestured towards the end of the corridor. They followed her all the way to the stairs and down through the reception, where they found a man with crustacean –like claws for hands, asleep behind the front desk. Galvina merely mouthed the word 'Sand' and opened the door, not bothering to do it quietly since the guard was far too deeply asleep to be disturbed. Once they were outside, Galvina quickened her pace as she led them down the empty street.

They had been walking briskly for about five minutes when Galvina turned down an alleyway.

'Ok guys, we can talk here for now. Are you all ok?'

'We're fine, thank you,' said Emily.

'That's good to hear. When Belactacus came and told me about the Council's decision, I feared the worst.'

'What do you mean?' asked Thomas, suddenly more concerned than ever.

'There are rumours about what goes on at the CFI. Nasty things that happen to Friends who refuse treatment. Seeing as you guys aren't Friends in the first place, I knew I had to get you out of there.'

'I spoke to a lot of the Friends …' said Emily slowly, 'None of them said anything about …'

'Well of course they wouldn't say anything,' said Galvina with a hint of exasperation, 'they're treated fine as long as they co-operate. It's those that don't that get …well, the rumours don't bear thinking about. Believe me, you're better off out of there.'

'Why didn't Belactacus tell us about any of this? He just let them take us!' said Thomas through gritted teeth.

'His …his hands were tied, Thomas …' said Galvina, unable for a moment or two to look Thomas in the eye. 'Anyway, the important thing is that you're out now!'

'Where are we supposed to go?' asked Isaac.

'I've arranged somewhere safe for you to stay the night. Follow me.' After checking that there was no one around, Galvina led them further down the street, looking round every corner along the way. They walked on for an hour until Isaac began complaining of all the things ten-year-old boys normally complain about when walking. Galvina assured him they were almost there, and began explaining what 'there' entailed as they walked. 'I know a few people who work in the Tower of Realms, and one of them did a little digging in the records for me. You see, they keep a record of every person who enters our Realm, every Hero, every Friend, everyone.'

'Like a census,' said Emily out of the blue.

'What's a census?' asked Isaac.

'Shut up, Eyes,' said Thomas.

'Wherever possible they record who Imagined them in the first place, and we managed to track down an old friend of yours, Emily. Literally an old Friend. Ah, we're almost there!'

They had entered a long street full of houses, as mismatched and odd looking as the rest of the city. Thomas saw a sign on the corner of one of the houses that read 'Bum Avenue'. He stopped to look at it again, thinking that the poor light and his fatigue had caused him to misread it. He was, however, right the first time. The sign indeed read 'Bum Avenue'. Galvina saw what he was looking at and smiled.

'This street is well known for housing some of the more …uh, unusual Friends. Everyone gets their own house or flat once they've integrated into, well, society I suppose.' Galvina then turned her attention to the house numbers as they walked, until they came to '22'. Once again she looked around before knocking at the door of a three storeyed house. Even in the darkness, the children could tell the house had been painted in a bright colour. A few moments later, they heard the sound of a key in a lock and the door opened. Thomas was most surprised to see it was a girl who had answered the door. She didn't look any older than he did. She had obviously been asleep, for her long ginger hair was pointing in a number of directions. She was wearing a spotty nightdress and the dopiest of looks on her face.

'Wha …wha …whaddya want?' she yawned.

'Georgie, it's me! Galvina! Let us in, quick!' Without waiting for an answer, Galvina ushered the children inside. They found themselves in a little kitchen and dining room, which to Thomas' mind was decorated as though it were the inside of a Wendy House. As Galvina turned on a small light, they could see that almost every surface was covered in remnants of dry paint. They could also see that Georgie was just as dishevelled as she had looked in the dark. Suddenly, Emily let out a gasp.

'I know you!' she exclaimed.

'I know you, too!' shouted Georgie, seeming to wake up rather quickly. Galvina shushed them immediately. She looked altogether very nervous.

'Emily, how do you know her?' asked Thomas.

'She was my imaginary friend, I made her up when I was six! Georgie Big Pants! She looks just how I thought she would …'

'Well, that's kinda the point!' said Georgie, rushing over to look more closely at Emily. 'You've grown!'

'So have you! I mean, I always imagined you being older than me. It was like having an older sister.'

From over at the dining room table, Isaac let out a derisive snort, perhaps louder than he had intended because everyone was suddenly looking at him.

'Personally, I've never seen the point in making up pretend friends. Not when I've got real ones.'

'Liar,' snapped Thomas. 'You've never made a proper friend and you know it.'

'I've got more online friends than you, Tommy!'

'Friends are usually people you've actually met and who actually like you, Eyes!'

'Just who are these two jokers?' asked Georgie, looking thoroughly amused.

'My cousins,' sighed Emily, as though she was pained to admit it.

'Just why are we here, anyway?' demanded Isaac, not taking his eyes off his brother.

'We're here because Georgie is Emily's imaginary Friend,' said Galvina, who had been looking out of the small kitchen window. 'We'll all go back to the Tower of Realms tomorrow and confront the Council. With Georgie testifying they'll have to believe that you're Real.'

'They weren't all that willing to listen to us before, why should they even let us in the door this time?' asked Thomas. 'Come to think of it, won't they just send us right back to the CFI once they find out we're missing?'

'Belactacus said it to me himself, we need to get you guys home,' replied Galvina insistently. 'Proper procedure and appeals will take too long, in fact they probably won't work at all. First thing in the morning, we take a train right back to the Tower of Realms and demand to see them. If we're lucky, by the time they realise you're not in your rooms at the CFI, we'll already be before the Council. In the meantime, how about we get some sleep?' Thomas couldn't help but think of this plan as very bold, which endeared it to him greatly and let him know he had been right about Galvina. She was the only one who really had their best interests at heart and actually had the nerve to do what needed to be done. He set about getting ready to go back to sleep secure in the knowledge that things were finally going right.

Georgie did not have much in the way of spare beds, or bedding for that matter, but they made do with what blankets and pillows she could find. Galvina said she'd stay awake by the front door, just to be on the safe side. Thomas and Isaac set themselves up in the tiny living room after a great deal of arguing over who got the sofa and who got the floor. In the end, Thomas was so tired he gave in and let Isaac sleep on the sofa. Emily went upstairs to sleep with Georgie. For the first time since arriving, Thomas felt confident and content as he fell asleep. At last, they had found definite proof that they weren't imaginary, and if all finally went to plan they might be on their way home by tomorrow afternoon. Thomas' peaceful sleep was disturbed a few hours later by the sound of a tremendous crash. Another one came as he sat bolt upright. It sounded distant, but not distant enough for comfort. Now he could hear screams coming from outside. The door to the living room was thrown open and Galvina came running in.

'Get up! Get up! We've got to get out of here, now!'

Chapter 11

The Attack

While Galvina dashed to the bottom of the stairs and shouted up to the girls, Thomas and Isaac went through the kitchen and opened the front door. The sun was just coming up and the street was a good deal busier than it had been the previous night, mostly due to the crowd of screaming, terrified Friends fleeing in every direction. Most were still in pyjamas or dressing gowns. They could hear more crashes coming closer, as well as roars and snarls and other terrible noises. They were pushed roughly from behind as Galvina came running out, Georgie and Emily right behind her.

'Whatever happens, stick together and follow me!' bellowed Galvina over the cries and screams of those around them. She began running down the street and naturally the others followed her, dodging panic-stricken people everywhere, fear on every kind of face. As they ran, Thomas kept looking around to see if he could see the source of all the trouble, when he suddenly got his first hint. There were renewed screams all around them, as from out of the sky came an enormous boulder. It soared through the air and then collided with the houses across the street from Thomas and the others. Rubble and debris were scattered all around. Some people were caught in the dust cloud and disappeared from sight entirely. Amid all the yells, they could hear the terrible animal-like sounds getting closer. Galvina urged them onwards, grabbing hold of Isaac's hand and pulling him along as she ran.

As they reached the end of Bum Avenue, they were met by a huge new crowd of fleeing people. They were upon them like a tidal wave before they could do anything about it. Galvina and Isaac were swept away from the others, while Georgie, Emily and Thomas struggled just to stay together. Shouting each other's names, they were jostled back and forth. Thomas tried to fight his way through to the side of the street but was knocked down by a great, hairy creature. Hitting the pavement hard on his side, he struggled to get back up again. He was certain he was going to be trampled to death when a hand reached down and grabbed hold of him, hoisting him up. Too dazed to see his rescuer at first, Thomas merely let whoever it was guide him away from the running crowd. Slumped against a wall, Thomas finally looked up to see that it had been Clark who had rescued him. Georgie and Emily were standing by him, looking more than a little shaken but not harmed. Thomas forced himself to stand up properly as Clark hollered over the din.

'No time to explain, we have to ...' Before Clark could finish, however, his jaw went slack at the sight of what had just come charging down the street. An enormous creature that looked like a rhinoceros, only with far too many horns, was rampaging towards the retreating crowd. Above it were several flying monsters. They had ghoulish faces, sharp claws and scrawny bodies. While the rhinoceros monster charged on, these harpies flew back and forth across the streets, attacking individual stragglers. When one of them spotted Clark and the children, it let out a loud, piercing shriek. Instantly the others turned, swarming towards the children. There was nowhere to run, nothing to pick up and use as a weapon, so Thomas did the right and noble thing. He grabbed hold of Emily and turned her away from the oncoming creatures, using his own body as a shield. He closed his eyes and waited for the claws to sink in. Beneath him, he could feel Emily moving her arm. Thinking she might be trying to break away, he only held her closer.

There came several other, more distressed shrieks, followed by the sound of several bodies colliding with the ground. Keeping hold of Emily, Thomas looked up to see what had happened. The harpies were all on the ground, writhing uselessly. It looked as though their wings had suddenly been frozen solid, glazed over with a heavy and powerful frost. Unable to fly or even stand, the creatures continued to shriek and scream, flailing their arms and legs.

'Come on, this way!' shouted Clark as he began to run away from the downed harpies and across the street. Thomas, Emily and Georgie followed him through the city, stopping to hide whenever they saw some monster stampeding through the streets.

'What's going on?' demanded Thomas.

'The Monsters have attacked. I have to get you out of the city,' gasped Clark as he endeavoured to catch his breath. 'We have to …keep going!' Unfortunately for Clark and the children, there was no quick way out of the city. They were forced to dodge more Monsters, trying their best to ignore the screams that became dimmer as they got closer to the edge of the city. Here and there some of the citizens of Impossible City had managed to get as far as them and continued to flee beyond the outskirts, where the buildings gradually gave way to open fields and small hills. It was from the top of one of these hills that Clark and the others were able to look back for a moment.

Under other circumstances, Thomas would have been in awe at the vast size of the city and marvelled at how even from here, the Tower of Realms could be seen. Right now, however, his sole focus was the gigantic Monsters continuing their attack, laying waste to buildings and pursuing the citizens. Fires were spreading everywhere, as dragons swarmed over the rooftops.

'Look, over there!' gasped Emily. She was pointing to her right, to a large domed building in the distance.

'That's the Library!' exclaimed Georgie. Thomas hadn't thought to look at the outside of the Library during their trip to the Tower of Realms. A number of giant Monsters could be seen attacking the walls of the Library. Clark forced them all to look away and pointed towards the distant horizon. 'There's a valley a few miles away. Hopefully we'll be safe there for a while.'

'What about Isaac? We can't just leave him behind!' said Thomas.

'Right now, my priority is to keep you safe. It's far too dangerous to go back into the city! If he's managed to escape, he'll hopefully have the sense to follow the others who have escaped. They'll all head for that valley at first.'

'Why?' demanded Thomas sharply.

'The army has an encampment there. We'll be safe,' asserted Clark, though he didn't look too sure of what he was saying.

As they got closer to the valley, Thomas couldn't help but notice the distinct lack of any Heroes, marching towards the city to help repel the attacking Monsters. He said nothing though for fear of upsetting Emily. He needn't have been so concerned, however, as she had noticed it as well, but didn't say anything in case she upset Thomas.

After much walking, they came to a steep incline that marked the entrance to the vast valley. Thomas and Georgie were the first to reach the top. Clark called from behind them that they should be able to see the camp. Neither Thomas nor Georgie had the heart to tell him what they could see. Torn down fortified walls, tents ripped to shreds, supply cases smashed and most terrible of all, bodies strewn across the ground. Clark's face fell as he reached the top of the incline and Emily let out a little gasp. The only blessing was that there was no sign of any Monsters. The attackers had made quick work of the camp and moved on to join the assault on the city. As Thomas and the others walked down into the valley they could see small figures moving slowly around the camp. Thomas was suddenly grabbed from behind.

'Just a minute, we can't just stroll down there!' gasped Clark. 'We don't know who or what they are!'

'Well they hardly look like Monsters, do they?' said Thomas. Clark began shaking his head frantically.

'You don't understand! They might not be what they seem …' Thomas merely snorted in exasperation and strode on towards the remains of the camp. Upon closer inspection the figures turned out to be fellow survivors from the city, who had come to the valley hoping for protection.

'Hey, hey you!' cried one of the survivors as he saw Thomas and the others approach. 'You …you work in the Library, don't you?' He pointed a shaking finger at Clark. 'What's going on? Are the Heroes in the city? Where are they?'

'Calm down, Jonah!' said a young lady next to the hysterical Friend. 'They probably don't know any more than we do. It's obvious they only just got out of the city with their lives.' She left Jonah's side and approached Clark. 'My name is Hannah. Jonah's right, you do work at the Library, don't you?'

'Yes, yes I do,' said Clark quietly. 'I'm afraid we don't know anything more than the rest of you. We got caught up in the attack and fled the city.' Emily stepped forward and introduced herself, which of course is the proper thing to do in a crisis.

'How many others have made it here?' she asked Hannah.

'A few, but no more than a dozen or so,' said Hannah. 'The Monsters were ruthless. They killed so many …they were all around us …then it was as though they were herding us, driving us back into the city. Pablo, Tumrug and Felix …they tried to slip out of the city with us but they were caught …and I don't know …' Hannah dissolved into tears and Emily quickly came to her side to comfort her, again as it was the proper thing to do. Thomas, however, turned his attention to Jonah.

'Are there no Heroes around at all?'

'Oh, they're around,' said Jonah darkly, 'but they're in no condition to fight. It seems most of them died in their tents when the Monsters came. Some look as though they were trampled. The rest are dotted around the camp.'

'Are any of them left alive?' asked Thomas, though he pretty much already knew the answer.

'No. I wasn't exaggerating when I said they're in no condition to fight. Like Hannah said, the Monsters were ruthless.' This provoked renewed tears from Hannah, and a dark look from Emily aimed at Jonah, as though his insensitivity were the root of all ills in the world.

'Now where are we supposed to go?' demanded Thomas, turning on Clark who stammered and fretted, obviously at a loss as to what to do. Fortunately for Clark, a familiar voice answered for him.

'We gather up whatever supplies are left and head for the mountains.' They all looked around, startled by the sudden, commanding voice that belonged to Belactacus. He was walking with a slight limp, his normally pristine clothes were ripped and dust-ridden. His hair was matted in places but the rest of it was more unruly than usual. In his hand he held a long, slim sword which was stained with drying blood. Emily rushed to him and hugged him, causing him to wince slightly. Thomas stayed exactly where he was.

'How did you get out of the city?' he asked slowly.

'By using my wit, wisdom, cunning and occasionally this,' said Belactacus, holding up the sword. 'The city has been overrun, and I can see that the garrison here was unable to stop them. It's good to see that some of you managed to escape, but where is Isaac?'

'Last time we saw him he was with Galvina,' said Emily, still staying very close to Belactacus.

'What were you all doing with Galvina in the first place?' asked Belactacus. 'We received word from the CFI that you had disappeared.'

'Galvina came and got us out of there,' explained Thomas, a steely edge in his voice. 'After you told her where we were, she came and took us to Georgie's house ...see, she was concerned because of all the horrible things that go on in the CFI. Care to tell us about some of them?' For the first time since they had met him, Belactacus looked confused.

'Firstly, there are no horrible things going on at the CFI. Secondly, I never got a chance to tell Galvina where you were, nor would I have. As a matter of fact, I have not seen her at all since we escorted you to the Tower of Realms. Clark, did you say anything to her?'

'No, sir,' said Clark. 'I was with you the entire time until we heard that the children were missing. I haven't seen Galvina since yesterday morning, same as you ...sir.'

'Then someone else must have told her and she lied to us,' said Emily.

'Either that or they're lying,' sneered Thomas, gesturing towards Clark and Belactacus. Georgie and Hannah looked shocked at the very idea, while Emily seemed unsettled. Belactacus, on the other hand, stepped away from Emily and moved towards Thomas, who didn't take his eyes off the sword for a moment. Belactacus stopped a mere step away from Thomas making no move to raise his weapon.

'I have just fought my way out of a city that has been my home for countless years. I have left behind the Library that I have worked extremely hard to maintain. Many of my friends and colleagues are likely dead. Believe me when I say to you, Thomas Llewellyn, that I have no reason to lie to you.'

'You've lied to us before!' shouted Thomas, not in the least bit intimidated.

'Oh really? Just what have I lied to you about?'

'There are plenty of things you clearly haven't told us about!'

'That is not the same as lying. I have kept some things from you for your own good because you are children. From the moment I learned of your presence in our Realm I have tried my best to get you out of it again by the quickest possible means, and that has meant keeping you in the dark about some things. For that, I shall not apologise.'

'I don't want an apology, I want ...' began Thomas, but Belactacus had no intention of arguing further.

'Now, why doesn't someone with a calmer head on their shoulders tell me what happened to you all after you left the Council chamber yesterday?'

At this, Belactacus turned from Thomas to Emily, who shakily recounted everything that had happened. She explained how Galvina had appeared in their rooms at the CFI in the middle of the night, she told Belactacus how Georgie was her old imaginary Friend and that Galvina had brought them to her so that she could come with them back to the Council. She then told him about the attack and how they had escaped, but Thomas noticed that she left out the part about the harpy creatures and how they had been stopped in their tracks. Thomas told himself that she must have been too panic-stricken at the time to have taken it in, though perhaps there was some other reason. Belactacus sat on a boulder and listened carefully to everything Emily said, asking no questions at all. When she had finished, he stood up slowly.

'Clark, round up all the other survivors you can find and instruct them to gather up any supplies we can use. It's a long journey to the mountains, but we cannot stay here.'

'What about Galvina and the other human child?' asked Clark.

'I'm afraid we cannot wait for them. Besides, I fear Galvina is no longer to be trusted. No arguments, young Thomas! We will do everything possible to recover your brother but we must do so from a place of safety and strength.

We shall travel along the valley and out the other side, then across the plains and into the woods at the foot of the mountains themselves. Hurry, gather what you can!' Once again, it seemed pointless to argue.

'The mountains!' breathed Jonah as they went about gathering supplies. 'He's not joking when he says it's a long journey! It's right out in the open, too! There's no cover or shelter for miles!'

'That may well be,' said Hannah, 'but don't forget Belactacus has been around longer than any of us. If we can't trust him right now, who can we trust?'

Thomas had been in earshot of both Hannah and Jonah, and the issue of trust was one that weighed heavily on his mind. While he was naturally concerned for his brother, one of Belactacus' comments kept ringing in Thomas' head. He had justified telling them so little because they were "children". This had been the attitude of almost everyone they had met since they arrived. He and his family were 'only children' and therefore needed looking after and talking down to. The only one who had treated them like adults had been Galvina and now Thomas was expected to believe that she was somehow working against them. She had taken them to a place of safety and had endangered her own life in trying to help them escape when the Monsters attacked. As they loaded what little supplies they could find into bags and began the march out of the camp and across the valley, Thomas didn't know who to trust anymore.

Chapter 12

The First Attempt

Isaac woke slowly, his senses returning to him one at a time. First came his hearing, but what he could hear terrified him. All around were growls, cackles and shrieks. Despite his better judgement, he opened his eyes but all he could see were blurry moving shapes. As his vision cleared, he shut his eyes again, for now he could see the source of all the terrible sounds. He was surrounded by Monsters. Goblins, ghouls, wolves, bogeymen and a number of creatures he had no name for, but they were no less terrifying for it. He tried to run, but it was only now that his sense of touch returned only to tell him that he was restrained. He could feel rope around his wrists and his chest. He guessed he was sitting in a chair and tied to it. Suddenly he felt hot, stinking breath on the back of his neck. One of the monsters had moved right up behind him. He just knew it was about to bite his head off. Keeping his eyes closed, he winced and tried to ready himself. He tried his best to choke back a sob. Then there came a loud shout and whatever it was behind him seemed to retreat. Isaac felt something touch his chin. Not slimy or scaly, but soft and human-like. He opened his eyes to find Galvina crouching down in front of him.

'Hey there, little bud! How are you feeling? Good to see you're awake already. I only gave you a pinch of Sand.'

'W-What? I don't understand!' whimpered Isaac, trying to focus on Galvina's face and not the multitude of Monsters standing a few feet behind her. It was then that a smile appeared on Galvina's face. Not her usual cheery smile, but a cruel and mocking one, which scared Isaac even further.

'You'll understand soon enough,' said Galvina as she stood up and walked away from him. Isaac could see now that he was in the middle of a large, circular room. His chair was placed facing a set of double doors. All around the room, windows had been boarded up in an effort to keep out as much light as possible. The Monsters continued to snarl and snicker, until the doors were suddenly thrown open and every creature in the room fell silent. Isaac was ecstatic to see Councillor Torvik stride into the room.

'T-Torvik! Help me! Get me out of here!' he yelled.

'A "please" wouldn't cost you much,' said Torvik casually as he walked towards Isaac.

'Please! Please help me!'

'That's much better,' said Torvik. 'It doesn't mean I'm going to help you escape, but at least I've managed to teach you some manners.' A low snicker rippled through the gathered Monsters. Isaac was dumbstruck as Torvik turned to Galvina. 'Where are the others? The older boy and the girl?'

'We became separated during the attack. I couldn't find them again and this one was making a hell of a lot of fuss, so I used the Sand and brought him here.' Torvik didn't look altogether too pleased at this, but he turned to one of the flying Monsters.

'Have all your fellows search the city.' The Monster, a large hawk-like creature with dirty, bedraggled feathers bowed low before walking out of the room. The scratching of its claws on the floor was soon replaced by the sound of flapping wings as it took off down the corridor. One of the Bogeymen dragged itself forward from the crowd of Monsters.

'Why look for the other humans? Surely we only need this one?'

'Fool!' snapped Torvik, causing the Bogeyman to cringe. 'We can't have two human children roaming freely around our Realm. Besides, what if something were to happen to this one? We may need a back-up.' Another round of laughter came from every Monster, punctuated here and there by a shriek or a bark. Torvik held up his hand for silence, which came instantly. Isaac was breathing heavily now, panic beginning to settle in for a prolonged visit and what he saw next did nothing to get it to leave. The Bogeyman who had spoken to Torvik suddenly looked stricken, as though in great pain. It let out a strangled cry and then, quite simply, faded away. The Bogeyman's sudden disappearance did not go unnoticed, as the Monsters began mumbling amongst themselves.

'A pity,' said Torvik, raising his voice above the collective murmur, 'but a profound reminder of why we must do this.' If Isaac wasn't confused before, he certainly was now. Had Torvik done something to the Bogeyman, perhaps to punish him, or was it something else altogether?

'Just what are you going to do to me?' asked Isaac, his entire body trembling beneath the ropes.

'Can I give him another dose of Sand?' asked Galvina, her hand itching towards a pouch tied to her belt. 'Shut him up?'

'No, unfortunately we need him to be conscious. Find something to gag him with.' Smiling terribly, Galvina produced a large handkerchief from her pocket and tied it around Isaac's mouth. He tried to struggle against it and call out, but he stopped when he heard a loud, fast clicking coming from the corridor outside. Almost moving too fast to see, an enormous cockroach came scuttling into the room, crawling along the wall. Its clicking became faster, as though it was talking.

'He says he and the other Crawlies have searched the city but there's no sign of the other three Councillors,' translated another Bogeyman.

'Never mind, they can't do anything to stop us now,' said Torvik confidently, striding back and forth across the space in front of Isaac. 'We have everything we need to begin the invasion right here. We have our entire army behind us and most importantly of all, we have the child! The human child!' At this, the crowd of Monsters cheered. Torvik threw up his arms, exulting in his triumph. 'We shall all go through together as the advance party and establish a foothold in the Realm of Reality, followed swiftly by the rest of our forces! We shall overwhelm the humans, find the Caretaker and destroy it! Reality and destiny await us all!'

The Monsters had all cheered throughout this little speech, but now as Torvik approached Isaac, they fell silent once more. Every hideous eye was fixed on them. Isaac's own eyes were wide with fear, shifting from Torvik's face to his hand as it came up and closer to Isaac's head. At first Isaac thought it was a trick of the light, or perhaps he was going mad, but Torvik's hand seemed to shimmer and fade as it got closer. The Councillor's face was set in deep concentration as he touched Isaac's forehead. It was a touch that Isaac did not feel, but he felt what came next. Torvik's transparent hand seemed to pass through Isaac's flesh and bone, straight through into his very brain and the mind contained therein. All at once, Isaac felt such tremendous pressure inside his head. Every nerve was on fire, waves of agony rippled throughout his mind. He could not cry out, not because of the gag, but because his brain could not carry out a task as complex as screaming when it was under such a direct attack. He could not even wish for the pain to stop, so great was the disruption to his thoughts. Suddenly, he could feel the pressure beginning to ease and though his vision was blurry, he could just discern the figure of Torvik reeling backwards. Another blurred figure rushed to his side but was roughly pushed away. The room was still silent but for the heavy breathing of both Isaac and Torvik.

'What's wrong? What happened?' asked Galvina, genuine fear in her voice.

'You …you brought the wrong child!' gasped Torvik, struggling to regain his composure. He managed to stand up straight, his hateful gaze not leaving Isaac. 'He is Un!'

Another collective murmur went up amongst the Monsters. Galvina, trembling all over, backed away from Torvik.

'I didn't know! I couldn't have known!' she protested.

'I see that now. It is a setback, but we can overcome it,' said Torvik, turning away from Isaac, who was far too dazed to even begin to understand what was happening.

'Are …are you alright?' Galvina asked Torvik, taking him by the elbow. He immediately and violently pulled away.

'Do not concern yourself …I just wasn't expecting to encounter such difficulty from the boy's mind. When we have one of the others it will be much easier.'

'What shall we do with him?' asked Galvina, now glaring coldly at Isaac.

'Have him locked away under heavy guard. Round up all surviving citizens and hold them in the Central Square. The other two human children are out there somewhere. Find them! Everything depends on it!' Torvik strode from the room, his hand held against one side of his head. The Monsters all shied away as he left. Galvina motioned for something behind Isaac to take him away, which is precisely what it did. The cords that bound him were cut away then a set of huge, rough hands grabbed him from behind and carried him out of the room. Isaac's sight was still poor from his gruelling experience, but at least that meant he couldn't really see the drooling, pig-like face of the Monster carrying him. He could only feel himself being jostled about as it walked, the corridors and stairs it took him down being nothing more than passing shapes.

Soon enough he found himself on a hard, cold floor. He heard a door being locked and a loud grunt as the Monster strolled away. There was little light, but Isaac did not want to see. He did not want to hear, smell or feel anything in this wretched nightmare. He would, however, have given anything for a loving hug, or a friendly touch of any kind. It was then that he felt something grasp his shoulder gently and he recoiled in shock, gasping desperately.

'It's alright …I won't hurt you …it's …it's Isaac, isn't it? That's your name? I'm so sorry, Isaac …I'm sorry I didn't believe you …'

Chapter 13

Names and Lies

Ever since they had left the ruined camp, Thomas had kept Belactacus in his sight. The journey along the valley so far had been long, uneventful and dull. At least it had been for Thomas. Emily seemed to be quite enjoying herself, as she kept asking Belactacus about the various unfamiliar birds and animals they could see. Strange animals that had been thought up by people but not allowed to return to the Realm of Reality. This had included a sighting of a Popolopagus, which turned out to be a sort of cross between a cow and a chicken that farted purple bubbles. Thomas only cared that it was harmless and not a threat. Nothing mattered to him other than getting his little squit of a brother back and getting home. He wiped the sweat from his forehead with the back of his hand and resumed his hard stare at the back of Belactacus' head, who was chatting pleasantly to Emily as they walked.

'She always was curious,' said a voice to his left that turned out to be Georgie. 'Always wanting to know what things were, driving her parents half mad with questions. I think they started buying her all those books so she could maybe get answers from them instead!'

'How do you know so much about her?' asked Thomas.

'I came from her imagination. I know her just as well as she knows herself … or at least I used to.'

'What do you mean by that?'

'It's like this …when a child thinks up an imaginary friend, we're instantly pulled into this Realm but we sort of remain connected to the child. When they think of us playing together, which is what they imagine us for in the first place, we are there with them …and yet we're not. We see them in our mind's eye just like they see us in theirs. Then, eventually, they stop thinking about us and we …well, move on with our own lives, I suppose. We never forget our human child, but more often than not they forget about us.'

'What do you do after they …you know, forget?'

'Oh, we pretty much live our own lives. Me, I like to paint.'

'Yes, I did notice,' muttered Thomas, thinking of all the various paint stains around Georgie's house. That in turn got him thinking about the distinct possibility that Georgie's house may have been destroyed in the attack. He quickly did his very best to stir the conversation in another direction. Any direction whatsoever.

They talked some more as they walked, mostly about Thomas and his life in the Realm of Reality. Georgie was incredibly curious about what Real teenagers did. It was only then that Thomas noticed that Georgie was closer to his own age than Emily's. Georgie had been older than Emily when she had first been Imagined, as Emily had often wondered what it was like to have an older sibling or indeed any kind of sibling. Georgie certainly didn't dress like any of the girls Thomas knew, not that he knew many. Moreover, none of the girls he knew had ever talked to him like this. Georgie took a genuine interest in him, whereas most of the girls at his school barely acknowledged his existence.

'So, just gonna throw this out there …why do you use your full name?' asked Georgie.

'Sorry?'

'I mean, why "Thomas" all the time? Why not 'Tom' or 'Tommy'?' Thomas couldn't help but wince a little at this question. It was, for him at least, a sore subject.

'It's just …I've never really liked being called Tom or Tommy …so I just prefer to use my proper name.' Georgie looked sideways at him, with every ounce of scepticism her face could express.

'It's more than that. Come on, tell me the truth.'

'Ok, ok! When I was little, my mum used to call me … "Tommy Tom Tom". One day at school one of the other boys, Robbie Crimshaw …heard my mum saying it and before you knew it every kid there was calling me 'Tommy Tom Tom'. Even one of the teachers started using it.'

'And no doubt this traumatised you for life?' ventured Georgie. 'Left deep emotional scars that haunt you to this very day and all that?'

'Oh, for sure,' said Thomas, fully aware he was being toyed with. 'You don't want to get involved with me, I've got issues.' Unable to keep straight faces anymore, the two sniggered and then laughed. It was the first time Thomas had laughed in a long time, and a nagging feeling at the back of his mind told him he may not laugh again anytime soon.

The laughter was cut short by a sudden, agonised cry that came from somewhere behind them. They turned to see one of the Friends clutching his chest, being supported by Hannah. The Friend became weak at the knees and started to collapse, but before he could hit the ground he had disappeared entirely. Hannah knelt down at the spot where he would have been and Jonah came up to grasp her shoulder.

'What happened?' whispered Thomas to Georgie, who looked just as saddened as Hannah and Jonah.

'There's no other way to put it,' she said softly, 'he died. That is, whoever Imagined him died. We live only as long as the person who Imagined us. When they die, we fade away. It usually happens quite suddenly, without much warning.'

'He …he didn't look all that old …does that mean …'

'Some Friends don't age as much as others, some don't age at all. It depends on the imagination of the human. Chances are whoever Imagined him lived a fairly long life …whatever that means. It's something we've learned to accept, not knowing when we'll just go like that. It's still very sad though.' Thomas could hardly believe his ears. He had assumed, from what Georgie had told him only moments ago, that once these imaginary friends got here they could live their own lives. As it turned out, they were tied to the very life force of whoever Imagined them, somebody who forgot about them long ago. Mortality is not something most fourteen-year-olds care to think about, and truly enough most humans never know when their time will come, but it seemed to Thomas that these Friends were stuck with a tough deal.

A few steps ahead of them, Belactacus called for everyone to take a rest. They had left the valley by now and were looking out at a vast grassy plain. In the distance, a forest could be seen standing at the foot of a range of mountains. Neither Thomas nor Emily were so well travelled in their young years that they had ever actually seen a mountain, but they had seen them in books and on the television. Nothing on Earth, however, could quite compare to the enormous, snow-capped mountains that stood so far in the distance from them now. It was to the base of these very mountains that Belactacus intended to lead the group. He had insisted on them stopping for a rest here, however, as there was no cover between the valley and the forest so they would have to be rested enough to travel at a faster pace. As they sat and passed around what few rations there were, Thomas deliberately sat himself close to Belactacus, who was once again in polite conversation with Emily.

'If we maintain a good pace, we can reach the forest by nightfall. Which is all to the good because it would be far too dangerous to travel at night. There are Sand dunes dotted around the plains, the very same Sand that the army used on your cousins. In the daylight we can see and avoid them.'

'I had been wondering where that Sand might come from,' said Emily. 'It really knocked …'

'What can we expect to find when we reach these mountains?' asked Thomas, very loudly and clearly so as to cut off what his cousin was saying. Emily threw Thomas a dark look and would have berated him for his rudeness had Belactacus not spoken first.

'We can expect to find a fortified encampment. On the other side of the mountains lie the Barren Thought Lands, the home of the enemy. The fort is the most formidable stronghold the army has. We should be safe there.'

'Really? What do we do if the fort has been taken? Just like the one in the valley. What then?' asked Thomas. Belactacus paused before answering, making a point of chewing and swallowing his mouthful of food.

'We shall use our initiative.'

'So, in plain English, you don't know?' said Thomas testily.

'Thomas! That's enough!' snapped Emily. 'Belactacus knows what he's doing.' Thomas fell silent and finished his rations. His cousin's blind faith in Belactacus was beginning to get on his nerves. It wasn't long before Belactacus called for everyone to prepare to move on. Clark kept scanning the skies every other minute and Thomas knew he was looking out for flying Monsters.

Unlike the journey through the valley, where everyone had travelled at their own speed, it was Belactacus who set the pace for crossing the plain. It was surprising just how quickly he could move. He didn't even slow down when a great herd of horses came galloping past the group, just a few hundred feet away. They were obviously wild but Belactacus and the other residents of the Realm of Imagination paid them no mind. Emily and Thomas, on the other hand, were amazed by them. They could only glimpse them as they rushed past, but it was clear that the horses were a vast range of different colours. Brown, black and white but also blue, red, green and purple among others. If they had had the time to really stop and watch them, they would also have seen the beautiful markings that made every single horse unique. As it was, they did not have time to stop and so could only watch ruefully as the herd disappeared into the distance.

Some time afterwards, Thomas began to struggle, but didn't wish to give anyone the satisfaction of seeing him struggle, especially not Belactacus. Emily put on the same façade, but rather because she didn't want to let down Belactacus than because of her pride. Georgie and Clark's faces were getting redder and redder all the time and one or two of the other survivors were beginning to lag behind. A few tried to suggest that they stop for a while, but gave up when it became clear that Belactacus was deaf to such requests. A few hours into their brisk jaunt, however, Belactacus began to slow down. Thomas took some satisfaction in catching up to him, delighting in the fact that this apparent swash-buckling Librarian did indeed have limits. Tired and more than irritable, all his grievances from the past few days had been simmering during the long walk and were now ready to boil over.

'Slowing down, old man?' said Thomas, only barely hiding his own breathlessness. Belactacus appeared to ignore him. 'That's right …just pretend I'm not here. That's what you've been doing ever since we arrived. "Just leave it to me, dear little children. I'll sort it all out for you while you go and play! Why not read a nice book?" Don't have that luxury anymore, do you? Stuck in the same crappy situation as us! Maybe it's time, then, that you started giving us some answers!'

'As I've already told you, Thomas, there are certain things you don't need to know,' said Belactacus calmly, not altering his pace for a moment.

'Yes! Yes, I do! You say you don't know how we got here in the first place, yet back at the Council chamber you claimed to be an expert in this, that and just about everything else! What aren't you telling us?' Normally Emily would have tried to intercede here, but she was at least two dozen paces behind them, struggling to keep going. She could, however, hear every word her cousin was saying. As could Belactacus, who actually slowed down a little.

'I meant what I said when I told you I don't know how you came to enter our Realm. I'm afraid it's the Council I was not being entirely truthful with.'

'Wait …what?' exclaimed Thomas.

'I intimated to the Council that your coming here may have been an accident. The truth is I suspect you were brought here on purpose.'

'On purpose?' spluttered Thomas. 'Who?'

'I'm afraid I really can't be sure,' answered Belactacus quietly, 'but I have my suspicions.' At this, Thomas reached out and grabbed Belactacus roughly by the arm.

'There you go again! You're never quite sure of anything, are you? You know what? I don't see any damn reason why I should trust you! You tell us just enough to try and keep us quiet and when it comes to the important stuff, you shut us out! I've had enough of it, you hear me? I've had …'

'Stop! Stop it!' shouted someone from behind Thomas. He spun round, ready to shout and bawl at just about anyone when he saw who had shouted at him. It had been Emily, and at this present time, she was levitating at least six feet off the ground.

Chapter 14

Learning of the Realm Maker

'Get her down, get her down quickly!' bellowed Belactacus, nearly pushing Thomas out of the way in an effort to get to Emily. Clark had been standing closest to her as they walked and was currently jumping up and down, trying to catch hold of her feet. Belactacus kept calling up to her, but she was staring straight ahead, her face bright red. She didn't seem to be aware of her current predicament. Thomas could only stand and watch, stuck firmly between shock and amazement. Then all of a sudden, Emily went entirely limp and came crashing down to the ground. Luckily Clark was just about able to catch her. Just as he did, one of the other escapees from the city let out a cry and pointed upwards. Thomas and the others all looked up to see three large flying creatures fairly high up and heading in their direction.

'We need to find cover!' exclaimed Clark.

'There isn't anything for miles!' said Georgie. Only she was wrong. Not twenty yards away, a collection of trees and bushes had materialised out of nowhere.

'That …that wasn't there a moment ago …' began Clark.

'Never mind, get under cover quickly!' ordered Belactacus. Thomas snapped himself out of his stupor and ran to help Clark support Emily as the entire group quickly took shelter among the trees and bushes. Luckily the trees seemed to provide enough shelter to hide everyone, and every last Friend crouched underneath them, quaking at the prospect of descending sets of claws. Only Belactacus and Thomas were watching the skies, tracking the movement of the flying Monsters. As they passed overhead, screeches could be heard, mixed in with the beating of large wings. The foul things flew on, and Belactacus let everyone know when they were out of sight. There was a collective sigh of relief from all except Emily, who was still unconscious.

While Clark and Georgie attempted to revive her, Thomas rounded on Belactacus. He either forgot that Belactacus had a sword or he didn't care as he roughly grabbed hold of the front of Belactacus' clothes. It was either surprising strength on Thomas' part or total lack of resistance from Belactacus that allowed the teenager to force the older man up against a tree. Several Friends let out exclamations of shock that were entirely ignored.

'Explanation. Now!' was all Thomas could say through firmly gritted teeth, pinning Belactacus to the tree. Belactacus made no move to resist or escape from Thomas' clutches. His sword remained at his belt, untouched.

'It was you …you and Emily …' said Belactacus softly.

'What the hell is that supposed to mean?' barked Thomas.

'She made herself float in the air like that …and I'd venture a guess that we have you to thank for the sudden appearance of these trees.' Thomas did not loosen his grip, if anything he tightened it as though to provoke further explanation. 'The trees on your world don't just give form to the things you imagine …they also give humans extraordinary powers. Whatever ability you can imagine for yourself becomes yours in earnest.'

'I don't believe you. If that were true, people would be imagining all sorts of powers for themselves …' began Thomas.

'Allow me to finish! There was a time when your people were aware of all this, or at least some of them were. The

112

ability is most profound in those who possess particularly strong imaginations. Long ago, certain humans came to harness these powers and used them for their own selfish gains. That's how myths of sorcerers and conjurers came to be so prevalent in your world's various cultures. They would manipulate kings, raise their own armies with a mere thought, set nation against nation. They were set on a course that would have torn your world apart.'

'So what happened? What changed?' asked Thomas, properly listening to Belactacus for the first time since that first discussion in the Library's kitchen.

'Release me and I'll tell you.' Thomas reluctantly let Belactacus go, who immediately straightened the front of his clothes. 'You won't find what I'm about to tell you in any of your world's history books, but that is entirely by design. Amid all the corruption and chaos caused by those who abused this power, one human decided to change everything. Nobody knows this human's name, or even if it was a man or a woman, but whoever it was, they came to be known as the Realm Maker. He or she set about imagining, and therefore creating, the entire Realm of Imagination.'

'You mean …this Realm wasn't always here?'

'Indeed not. It was created not only to store the figments of human imagination but also to curtail the imaginative powers of your race. All those so-called sorcerers lost their powers the moment this Realm was created.'

'If humans lost these powers …why do you think …' Thomas stopped himself as he remembered something. A conversation he wasn't supposed to hear. 'I heard you …I heard you talking to Torvik. You said we needed to be sent home before we became aware of what we could do …'

'Putting the sheer impoliteness of eavesdropping aside, you're quite right. The Councillors and I are some of the very few people who know what the presence of humans in this Realm means. Here, you have full access to the range of powers that your race was always meant to have. Here you can Imagine just about anything into existence, directly into this Realm. Remember when you asked me about the non-fiction books in the Library? The fact is we keep them under especially close scrutiny, for non-fiction deals in fact, and in the mind of a fully powered human, those facts can be rearranged. History, physics …time and space itself could become the plaything of one person. With an engaging, creative mind …there would be no limit to a person's power. They could become nothing short of omnipotent.'

Thomas had read and watched enough science fiction to know what that last word meant. All powerful. Able to do anything. The news came as an immense shock to him, this sudden realisation that he had the potential for such power. What scared him, however, was the fact that he didn't actually remember bringing the trees into existence. Then again, why would he? He didn't know he had this power at that point. It had clearly been a fortunately timed accident. As he cast his mind back, he thought of the clothes in his wardrobe back at the Library. Had he thought them up and therefore made them appear by accident as well? What else had he done without knowing? Belactacus seemed to be able to read all this in Thomas' face. He placed both hands gently on Thomas' shoulders.

'Thomas, let me make it very clear to you what this really means. While it can be argued that this power is entirely natural …the fact is humans are not ready to possess it. Imagine such power in the hands of humans today. Not just world leaders, but anyone. One person could cause more destruction with a single thought than all the greatest man-made weapons ever constructed. Your world is full of divisions, sides are taken and battles are fought over anything and everything. How long do you think your world would survive? Imagination is a wonderful gift, Thomas …but humanity is not ready for its full, unrestrained power.' Thomas nodded throughout Belactacus' speech, but his mind was elsewhere. He was turning his thoughts to the possibility of using these newfound abilities to rescue his brother. Certainly in order to get to Isaac he would have to fight his way through an army of Monsters, but what chance did they have against him? He could maim and destroy them without raising a finger. He suddenly became aware that Belactacus had finished speaking, so he tried to look very solemn and gave an especially grave nod of his head. Belactacus studied Thomas' young face for a moment or two, then said nothing as he left him to check on Emily. Thomas, naturally, came with him.

Clark and Georgie had succeeded in reviving Emily. She was understandably groggy and it took some time to explain to her what had happened. With Belactacus kneeling at her side, Emily then started to tell them what little she could recall from the past few minutes.

'I remember getting angry ...at you two,' she said somewhat sheepishly, looking at Thomas and Belactacus. 'You were shouting so much that I felt like I wanted to get away, far away.'

'And so you started flying,' said Belactacus bluntly, as though young girls frequently started floating above the heads of their friends. 'Emily, this is very important. Have you done anything like this before?'

'Yes ...' said Emily after hesitating for a moment. 'When we were getting out of the city. We were attacked by these horrible flying things ...I remember panicking and thrusting my hand out ...then their wings were frozen. I'm sorry I didn't tell you before ...I wasn't even sure what I'd done.'

'I had a feeling you were holding something back, but I understand. It would frighten anyone,' said Belactacus before standing up. 'Clark, make sure everyone is alright, and tell them we'll be heading for the forest immediately. You'd best go with him, young Georgie.' Once Clark and Georgie were out of earshot, Belactacus turned to Thomas and Emily, the former of whom had helped the latter to stand up. 'Now, I need you both to understand something. The level of imaginative power I spoke of earlier takes a great deal of mental discipline and training. That being said, accidents can happen and people can get hurt. I would like you both to try, as best as you can, to suppress any fanciful impulses and generally be on guard.'

'We …we'll try,' said Emily quietly. As before, Thomas said nothing. He didn't believe in making promises he couldn't keep.

'I can ask no more of you,' said Belactacus kindly. 'Now, we should get ready to move on. If we're quick we can make the forest before nightfall.'

It was indeed beginning to get dark by the time they reached the edge of the forest. There wasn't a pair of feet in the entire group that didn't ache and only a handful of mouths that weren't complaining about it. As far as rations went, they had food but little water left. Much of it had been drunk during the crossing from the valley to the forest. Thomas made a joke about conjuring up some burgers, fries and a fizzy drink or two. Clark was the only one to hear it and gave Thomas a stern look in return.

Everybody set about making themselves as comfortable as possible as it was too far to the camp to risk travelling at night. They were unable to light a fire in case they attracted the attention of the enemy. Clark volunteered to stand watch first, which is to say Belactacus strongly suggested that he take the first watch and Clark didn't have the energy to object. Emily and Georgie were lying close together doing what girls quite often do before going to sleep, namely chatting. Thomas was lying nearby but wasn't even remotely inclined to join in the conversation. While everyone around him bedded down for the night, he felt wide awake. He was therefore fully alert when Clark came striding back to the group, having only been away for a few minutes.

'Clark? What is it? What's wrong?' asked Thomas.

'It is none of your concern, go to sleep,' said Clark bluntly. Biting back a retort that would no doubt have shocked his mother, Thomas hauled himself up and followed Clark. Clark looked back as he walked and for a moment it seemed he might insist that Thomas go back, but he merely shook his head and continued on. It soon became clear that he was looking for Belactacus, whom he found sitting with his back to a tree trunk.

'Back already, Clark?'

'Sir, I've found …someone. I think you should come and see.'

'Very well,' sighed Belactacus, using the tree behind him to help himself get up.

'Sir, perhaps Thomas should …'

'Oh no, I'm not being left out anymore,' said Thomas grimly, his eyes darting back and forth between Belactacus and Clark, wondering who would object first.

'I quite agree,' said Belactacus, surprising both Thomas and Clark. 'It is likely that you'll be with us for some time. It's only right that you be included. Come, show the way, Clark.' Thomas very nearly remarked on Belactacus' sudden change in attitude, but thought better of it and stepped back in order to let Clark pass.

Clark led them around the group, many of whom were now asleep, and through some dark purple bushes. They walked on down a small hill into a shallow, muddy ditch. Though the light was fading quickly, there was no mistaking the identity of their unexpected find.

'Councillor Gumm!' exclaimed Belactacus in genuine surprise. The Councillor's doughy green face turned to look up at Belactacus. There were tears in his eyes and he looked dirty and unkempt. His skin, if you can call it that, didn't look nearly as gelatinous as it had back in the Council Chamber. It now looked worn and almost hardened, like play dough that's been left out too long. He was still wearing the robes he had worn in the Council Chamber but now they were torn and filthy.

'Oh, Belactacus,' he moaned, his voice still deep but lacking the power it had had while the Council had been in session. 'You've found me. Oh yes …discombobulate.' While that last word made no sense to Thomas, Belactacus either didn't notice or knew precisely what was meant by it. In fact it visibly put him at ease.

'I'm sorry to say we weren't specifically looking for you, Councillor. You must have travelled hard, to reach the forest before us.'

'It's certainly been hard …but you see …I had a head start …' said Gumm, hanging his blobby head. 'I fled before the attack began …' Belactacus fell silent for a moment as the meaning of this sank in.

'Then you must have known about it beforehand,' he said darkly. 'Rather than alert the Council or the army, you decided to flee.'

'I couldn't …I couldn't!' sobbed Gumm, losing all pretence of control. 'I couldn't tell the Council …he has her! He threatened to kill her if I didn't do as he said! Don't you see? I couldn't tell them because he would know!'

'He's babbling,' muttered Clark dismissively.

'No, no he is not,' said Belactacus. 'He's referring to his wife, Humba. Gumm, what happened in the Fanciful Mountains?' This name jogged Thomas' memory right back to his late night eavesdropping. Torvik had mentioned the Fanciful Mountains and at the time Thomas assumed he was talking about one of the then mysterious Councillors. It turned out he was right, though it was hardly the time to point it out.

'Humba and I were exploring the mountains …I had climbed up to one of the peaks and when I turned around …she was gone …she had just vanished. I searched all over for her but couldn't find her. Then all of a sudden, I was set upon by a Monster …a Bogeyman! The foul thing told me my …my wife was their prisoner and that if I ever …ever wanted to see her again I was to get back to the Impossible City and …and do as I was told!'

'Do as you were told by whom?' pressed Belactacus, now kneeling in front of the distraught blob.

'Torvik! It was Torvik! The moment I arrived back he came to see me and said that if I didn't vote against the human children I would never see my poor Humba again!'

Chapter 15

Gumm Tells All

It took a great deal of effort to support Councillor Gumm up out of the ditch, up the hill and back towards the clearing where the others were trying to sleep. After his sudden outburst about Torvik, Gumm had turned into a gibbering, wobbling wreck. Clark fetched him a drink of water, which could be seen rippling down his throat as he drank it. It had a most rejuvenating effect, for his skin no longer looked quite so dry and rough. After this he began to calm down. Belactacus sat himself down on a tree stump directly opposite the Councillor.

'Now Gumm, what can you tell us about what Torvik is doing?' asked Belactacus.

'He wouldn't tell me much after I arrived back in the city. When I got to the Tower of Realms, I found him in my own personal chamber. I'd barely got a word out before he made the threat about my wife. What he did say was that it was vital that the three children appearing at the emergency session not be allowed to enter the Realm of Reality. Then he repeated his threat and …just left the room. I didn't see him again until we met with the rest of the Council.'

'What about afterwards? Did you speak to any of the other Councillors?'

'No ...after the session had finished they all went off in separate directions. I tried to find Councillor Milanda but she wasn't in her office or her chambers. None of her aides could tell me where she was either. I'd spent most of the day trying to find her and then decided to find Councillor Callion instead.'

'Remind me, which one was he?' asked Thomas.

'Councillor Callion is the army's representative on the Council. The rather large, stocky gentleman,' said Belactacus before turning his attention back to Gumm. 'You said you didn't get to speak to any of the Councillors.'

'I didn't. I was on my way to Callion's rooms when I passed an open door ...it was Torvik's office. It was getting dark by now and I don't think he saw me ...he was talking to a Bogeyman, Belactacus. A Bogeyman!'

'A Bogeyman? In the Impossible City?' said Clark, shock dripping from every syllable. 'That can't be ...the defences would have been up.'

'Not necessarily, Clark,' said Belactacus. 'The barrier doesn't go up until sunset, when Bogeymen can travel most freely. It comes down again at sunrise, but if Torvik is using the Bogeymen for some purpose, then obviously he would be providing them with sanctuary until they could escape the city.' Thomas chose not to ask anything at this point, but just assume that anything that involved a Bogeyman in a realm where the things humans imagine become real meant trouble.

'I could hear the Bogeyman and Torvik talking,' continued Gumm. 'The Bogeyman had come to tell him that the Monsters were poised ready to overwhelm the camp in the valley ...and that once the barrier came down in the morning ...they'd be able to start their attack and overwhelm the city.'

'Why didn't you warn someone?' asked Belactacus coldly.

'I'd already been trying to find Milanda and Callion! For all I knew Torvik had done something terrible to them and I ...I ...I panicked! I left the city as quick as I could and came out this way …I'm hardly proud of it, Belactacus, but it's what happened. No apology from me is going to change that.'

'I never expected one,' said Belactacus as he rose from the stump. He walked away a few paces, turning his back on Gumm, Thomas and Clark. He was silent for a few moments then turned to face them all. 'Gentlemen, let us start with what we know. We know that Torvik blackmailed Councillor Gumm into voting against you and your family, Thomas, despite assuring us he wanted to help you.'

'We also know he's in league with the Monsters,' added Clark.

'Indeed, and if he's been meeting Bogeymen, who can travel vast distances hopping from one shadow to another, then it seems likely that he's been in contact with the Monsters for some time now.'

'Then Torvik was behind the attack on the city?' ventured Thomas.

'Certainly. It seems he has managed to organise them in a way they could never do before. Ever since this Realm was created they've been a savage, unordered rabble. That's why the Heroes have had little trouble keeping them at bay.'

'But why? Why is he doing all this?' asked Thomas.

'This is purely a guess, but I can think of nothing else that would be worth all the trouble he has gone to. It seems he's after you,' said Belactacus, looking directly at Thomas.

Thomas felt the eyes of Clark, Gumm and Belactacus focusing entirely on him. For some reason unknown even to Thomas, the news didn't come as that much of a shock. Ever since they arrived, he and the others had been the focus of seemingly everybody's attention. Suddenly, although he wasn't sure how he could have forgotten it, Thomas remembered the earlier realisation about the powers being in the Realm allowed him.

'Do you think it has anything to do with …you know, what I can do? Is he after me for my powers?'

'I'm not so sure he's after you specifically,' said Belactacus softly. 'When I said he is after you, I should have said he's after you or Emily. If he's planning what I think he is, then almost any human child would suit his purpose.' Thomas was about to ask what that purpose was but Gumm spoke first.

'You don't mean …but he wouldn't …he'd be utterly mad to try …'

'He'd be mad to try without a human child, certainly …but with one, he would be sure to be successful.'

'Would someone mind telling me just what he's supposed to be trying?' enquired Thomas with an air of forced politeness.

'Remember what I told you, Thomas, about how being in this Realm removes the restrictions placed on your imagination? Well, the simple fact is that usually a human child is the greatest known source of imaginative power. As people get older they might retain some degree of imagination but it can never truly compare with what they had as a child. It is my belief that Torvik has somehow managed to engineer your arrival in the Realm of Imagination, or at least plans to take advantage of it. If he is able to acquire a human child, he can harness the imagination of that child and use it to open a portal to the Realm of Reality.'

'But you said that all five Councillors had to work together to do that,' said Thomas quickly, rather pleased with himself for remembering this.

'Usually, to create a stable portal, yes it would take all five Councillors. If any one Councillor attempts to do it alone the resulting portal would be …unstable, to say the least. Using the power contained inside a human child's mind, however, Torvik could open a stable portal alone.'

Thomas felt a sudden, sickening surge throughout his entire body. In all this, nobody had yet got onto the subject of Isaac and where he might be. If he was with Galvina and nobody seemed to trust her anymore, it seemed likely that she was working with Torvik.

'Don't you see? That's what must have happened to Isaac! Torvik's got him! By now he must have already …what the hell are you chuckling about?' snarled Thomas loudly, for Belactacus was not only smiling but beginning to laugh just a little.

'My apologies, Thomas, but I can assure you that your brother is in no danger of being used for whatever purpose Torvik has in mind. I knew it fairly soon after meeting him. Isaac is Un.'

'And just what is that supposed to mean?' snapped Thomas.

'It's what we call humans who are …well, unadventurous, unquestioning, uninterested and most of all, unimaginative. They're just …Un. Isaac does not possess enough of an imagination to be of any use to Torvik. He also won't have any access to the powers that you and Emily have already discovered. Ah, speaking of whom!' Thomas turned on the spot to find Emily and Georgie approaching from the makeshift camp.

'We heard shouting. What's going on?' asked Emily.

'We were this close to getting to sleep,' added Georgie grumpily.

'Your friend Torvik has been behind everything,' said Thomas, rapidly losing his temper. 'He and his Monster buddies have Isaac and even though apparently he's too 'Un' to be of any use to them, there's no telling what they've done to him!'

'Thomas, we cannot be sure what might be happening inside the city,' said Belactacus. 'For now all we can do is reach the army's headquarters and …'

'And what? Just what do you plan to do?' demanded Thomas. 'Suppose those Heroes go and storm the bloody city and Isaac gets killed in the process? What if he's been killed already? No …no! I'm done! Ever since we got here we've been shunted about, told not to worry and leave it all up to you lot because we're just children! I'm taking matters into my own hands! With these powers that you're all so afraid of, I can get into the city, rescue Isaac and destroy anyone and anything that gets in my way!'

'And there it is!' declared Belactacus loudly, looking down on Thomas with disgust. 'The desire to fight and destroy that makes the proud human race what it is today. This Realm has existed for thousands of years, curtailing the power of human imagination and just as I expected, nothing has changed. You are all far too ready and willing to use this power to wipe out those who oppose you. Aggressive, adversarial and barbaric!'

'At least I'm doing something here and now!' bellowed Thomas. 'By the time we get to this fort, Isaac could be dead!'

'Thomas …calm down, please!' pleaded Emily.

'He's your cousin, Emily! If you and I go now, we can get him back. Everyone here is afraid of us and what we can do, so I say we give them good reason to be afraid!' At this, Thomas barged past Clark, heading out of the forest. After a few steps, he turned back. 'Are you coming or not?' Despite the dark, he could see the look on Emily's face. Normally so confident and outspoken, she was currently at a loss for any words. She looked to Belactacus but he wasn't taking his eyes off Thomas, who in turn was staring intently at Emily. Clark and Georgie were trying to look at everyone at the same time. In the space of a few seconds, nothing and yet everything was said. Giving his cousin one final glare, Thomas turned and started walking away.

Normally a sensible grown up like Belactacus or possibly even Clark would have dashed after Thomas, grabbed him by the arm and brought him back for a stern reprimand. They both indeed made to do this, but something happened that nobody had counted on. Thomas' brisk pace had turned into a run, which became a sprint within seconds, which in turn became something else altogether. In a burst of accidental creative thought, Thomas considered how much he'd love to be able to just run far away from all of these idiots and suddenly became the fastest runner in all of creation. He didn't even hear Emily's shout as he burst forward and onward. Within seconds he was far away from her and everyone else in the forest.

Unfortunately, the thought was only fleeting which meant his newfound ability was too. He slowed down moments later, coming to a shuddering and uneasy stop, so uneasy that he lost his footing entirely and skidded to the ground. He lay there for a few moments then turned over onto his back. His face was hot from the painful fall, and upon reaching up to feel around his nose he discovered it was bleeding. The sudden burst of speed had come as much of a surprise to him as it had to the others, but it was over. Right now he was just a teenage boy on a dark, unfamiliar plain with nothing for company but the Monsters hunting in the darkness.

Chapter 16

The Second Attempt

While one brother had inexplicably hurled himself towards danger, the other already was and continued to be very much in danger. While the others had spent the day crossing the plain to the forest, Isaac had been sitting in a small, dark, cold room. It wasn't like a dungeon. The walls weren't stone or dripping wet. It was, however, bare. What little furniture there was had been removed by the Monsters to be used as materials to make barricades across various parts of the Tower and the city. The windows had been boarded up. In fact, all the windows in the Tower of Realms had been boarded up. Isaac had tried to pry the boards from the window in order to see outside and possibly escape, but his fellow prisoner pointed out that the room they were in was several storeys up and the window, if opened, would reveal only a sheer drop. Isaac's fellow prisoner knew this because she happened to be none other than Councillor Milanda, the head of the Reality Council. After Isaac had been thrown into the room with her and had been given a chance to recover from his ordeal at the hands of Torvik, he told Milanda everything that had happened to him since their hearing before the Council. She, in turn, told him a thing or two.

Unlike Councillor Gumm, Milanda hadn't become aware of Torvik's treachery until it was far too late. She apologised to Isaac over and over again for not believing him at the hearing, for she had voted against them not because someone was forcing her to, but because she genuinely believed them to be confused Friends. Milanda was not a woman to be manipulated if she could help it, but earlier that morning it had been made painfully clear to her that she had indeed been hoodwinked. Being an early riser, she was already at the Tower of Realms when the attack came. By the time the alarm sounded it was far too late and the Monsters had already swarmed deep into the city. What few Heroes were assigned to guard the Tower of Realms had made a valiant stand in the main courtyard, advising Milanda and everyone else who worked in the Tower to take shelter inside.

The Heroes fought bravely but ultimately fell to the Monsters' superior numbers. Milanda had gone straight to her chambers, only to find Torvik there. Naturally at first she assumed he was in just as much danger as she was, but that assumption changed when Torvik drew a sword and held the point directly at Milanda's heart. The Monsters entered the Tower to find their master holding a valuable prisoner. She had been roughly taken to this tiny room, where Isaac joined her a few hours later. Isaac had just about been able to tell her most of what Torvik had said to the crowd of Monsters, and what she heard disturbed her greatly.

'The Caretaker? He definitely said 'Caretaker'?'

'Yeah …yes, I think so,' said Isaac wearily. His mind wasn't so much on Caretakers and Monsters and invasions. He was thinking about Thomas and Emily and where they might be. It may have been virtually impossible for him to actually get along with his big brother, and his cousin was a bit of a dork, but they were the only family to be had in this entire Realm.

'He can't be planning to …it would be utter madness,' said Milanda, almost to herself.

'He said they were going to destroy the Caretaker …whatever that means,' said Isaac miserably.

'The destruction of the Caretaker will mean nothing short of the destruction of this entire Realm!' exclaimed Milanda, shocked at how casual Isaac was being. 'Didn't anyone at the Library or the CFI tell you about how this Realm was created and how it is maintained?' Isaac shook his head slowly, so Milanda went on to explain how the Realm was created, much the same way that Belactacus had explained it to Emily and Thomas. 'The Realm Maker knew that once he or she died, the Realm of Imagination would cease to be. So the Realm Maker found someone who could be trusted, someone who could be told all about the Realm of Imagination in great detail. That person became the first Caretaker, for as long as they had knowledge of our Realm, it would continue to exist and serve its purpose. Across the centuries, when they feel their lives are close to ending, each Caretaker has passed on the knowledge of the Realm to a new person. If Torvik does manage to track down and kill the current Caretaker …our Realm will cease to exist. Why would he …'

Suddenly there came the sound of a key in the lock and the door swung open. There stood a Bogeyman, flanked by what looked like two trolls, each of them carrying an armful of books. The foul stench of the trolls was overpowering. The Bogeyman strode into the room, grinning grotesquely and gestured for the trolls to place the books on the floor across from where Milanda and Isaac were sitting.

'Good afternoon, honoured Councillor and human child. A selection of books for the young man!' leered the Bogeyman, indicating the pile of books. 'Councillor Torvik strongly suggests you begin reading at once …do enjoy, won't you?' Letting out a soft, rasping laugh, the Bogeyman set a lit candle down on the floor and left the room followed by the trolls. Milanda held out her hand to keep Isaac quiet and still as she listened for the sound of the door being locked again. She waited a few moments, leant across to pick up a few of the books, then turned to Isaac.

'I'm going to assume that you're not a big fan of reading, Isaac?'

'Not really, no. I prefer video games.'

'You prefer what? Never mind. Under any other circumstances, I'd highly recommend most of these books. I have a feeling that Torvik wants you to read these so that you can exercise your imagination. He's hoping he might still be able to use your mind to open a portal.' Milanda stopped to think for a moment or five. 'Here's what we're going to do for now. You'll have to pretend to read them, look at the pages but try not to think about what is on them. Can you do that?'

'Sure. I do it at school all the time.' Milanda couldn't help but give a little smile as Isaac pulled the first book towards him and opened it at the first page.

For the next few hours Isaac just stared at page after page, not really taking in anything. This was a shame as the books included some of the best the human world has to offer. Whatever else Torvik was, he had good taste in books. It became harder and harder for Isaac to concentrate on not concentrating as nobody brought him anything to eat. However hungry and cold he became, he persevered with the task at hand, as it was all he had to do. Around mid-afternoon, the door opened again and the Bogeyman returned, this time accompanied by four other Monsters.

'Good afternoon,' drawled the Bogeyman. 'I trust you have been comfortable? Enjoying the books, are we?' This time Milanda stood up, and although drawing herself up to her full height made her no taller than the Bogeyman, it didn't mean she wasn't impressive.

'Kindly dispense with the false pleasantries, Bogeyman. What do you want?'

'We are here to escort you both to the Council Chamber. Our master is waiting there for you. You can either walk or be carried. Master Torvik did not say which he'd prefer ...'

'We shall walk, of course. Come along, Isaac. Let us not keep Master Torvik waiting.' Certainly not in the mood to argue, Isaac rose and walked alongside Milanda. They were soon flanked by the Monsters, the two trolls from earlier behind them while a large goblin-like creature and a snake with arms and legs walked in front of them. The Bogeyman led the way.

'He doesn't look much like a Bogeyman,' said Isaac quietly, nodding towards the Bogeyman. 'He almost looks human.'

'Not all of his kind look the way you expect them to,' replied Milanda just as quietly. Luckily the heavy footfalls, the low grunting of the trolls and the hissing breath of the snake covered their conversation. 'Those Bogeyman that look most like humans are, in fact, the more dangerous. They are false, cunning and capable of terrible acts. They are imagined into being by children who have good reason to fear the adults that are supposed to look after them and keep them safe. Not all Monsters look as terrible on the outside as they are on the inside, Isaac, in our Realm or yours.'

Upon reaching the Council Chamber, they found that all the desks had been removed including the raised desk the Councillors had sat at. There was at least a dozen Monsters dotted around the room, not nearly as many as there had been in the room Isaac had woken up in. Galvina and Torvik were standing in the middle, deep in conversation. Upon seeing the Bogeyman return, Torvik held up his hand to silence Galvina and strode forward to meet Isaac and Milanda.

'Ah, how good to see both our honoured guests! I trust you haven't been bored, Isaac?'

'Perhaps not bored, Torvik, but the poor child has no doubt been hungry!' snapped Milanda. 'Besides, you are utterly wasting your time sending him books. I saw through that in an instant. A few hours of reading will not instantly make up for a childhood spent messing about with gadgets and games. You'll find no quick fix to your problem there, Torvik.'

'Problem? Problem?' said Torvik, laughing good naturedly. 'I wasn't aware I had a problem.'

'Oh, I think you are all too aware of the dilemma you find yourself in. It is your newfound allies that you want to keep in the dark.' Milanda gestured broadly to the Monsters surrounding them. Isaac couldn't help but notice Torvik's face twitch slightly. 'Your grand scheme hasn't gone to plan. You expected to be in the Realm of Reality by now but you captured the wrong child, leaving you unable to open a stable portal. I can only hope the other two have found a place of safety.'

'What you call a problem, Milanda, I call only a minor setback,' said Torvik, loud enough for all in the room to hear. 'The other children will be found soon enough. I have more than enough forces to hold the city and still search for the humans out on the plains. You'd be surprised, Milanda, at just how many Monsters there are out there in the Barren Thought Lands. A vast army, with such immense potential. All they really needed was a leader. Someone with vision and intelligence.'

'And they ended up with you instead. My sympathies to you all,' said Milanda tartly to the Monsters. Despite everything he'd been through, Isaac let out a weak chuckle. Torvik, on the other hand, was not laughing anymore. He was still smiling though, which is never a good sign.

'What is it you've always said, Milanda?' asked Torvik. 'A good leader is someone who thinks on their feet and uses their initiative.'

'I've never said anything of the sort.'

'Haven't you? Well, perhaps I wasn't really paying attention. Council sessions tend to bore me. The point is I have certainly used my initiative in the face of this little setback. Not only are my forces scouring the area for the other children, but we're going to continue to try and open a portal here in the meantime. By myself.' At this, Milanda dropped all pretence. Her face fell as she saw the sincerity in Torvik's.

'You can't be serious …there's no way such a portal would be stable …'

'Perhaps not, but then again …I have to be seen to be trying or they'll lose confidence in me,' said Torvik quietly and smiling wickedly. Isaac didn't notice Galvina come up behind him and grasp him by both shoulders. Though he had managed to rest a little after his ordeal, he didn't have the strength to get away and he knew it. Therefore he did not attempt to resist. 'So, this is what's going to happen,' continued Torvik. 'I am going to open a portal right here. I can either use our young friend here in the hope that those books made him a little less Un …or you can help me, Madam Chair.'

'I …I beg your pardon?'

'Normally it takes all five Councillors to open a stable portal, but sadly for me the other three are not present at our impromptu session. They didn't even send apologies for their absence, isn't that just awful? If you and I work together, we might just be able to do it. Of course, if you're not on board, I'll have to get Isaac to help. He doesn't get a choice. You do, Madam Chair.' Milanda turned to look at Isaac. Even if he didn't look half-starved and exhausted, Milanda knew that he'd never survive a second attempt. As though able to sense what she was thinking, Torvik gestured for Galvina to bring Isaac forward, which she did with relish.

'No, stop!' shouted Milanda, moving to intercept Galvina and causing some of the Monsters to stir uneasily. She stared straight at Torvik, while he in turn kept his gaze very much on her. 'If you leave the boy alone, I will do what I can to help you.'

'The voice of reason as always, Madam Chair. Stand back, everyone!' shouted Torvik grandly, like a ringmaster at a circus. All the Monsters edged backwards until they were right up against the walls and Galvina, keeping a grip on Isaac, did the same.

Torvik and Milanda were now standing opposite each other. Isaac hadn't noticed them before, but in the space between where the desks used to be, the floor was marked. Around the circular space were five smaller circles marked with tiles. Milanda and Torvik were each standing on a circle, with three left vacant. They both held out their right hands, fingers outstretched.

'You realise, of course, that even if we manage to create a stable portal, we cannot be sure of where in the Realm of Reality it will open,' said Milanda, not taking her eyes off the centre of the circle.

'Duly noted, Madam Chair …just focus on stabilizing the portal itself,' said Torvik. 'Once it is stable, I can guide it to our chosen destination. I've become quite adept at manipulating the orientation of the portals. Not that anyone has noticed.'

'So that's how you brought Isaac and the others here …you hijacked the portal we all created to send that newt through and you …'

'…Created a sub-portal that locked in on a group of children particularly gifted in imaginative thought, yes,' said Torvik, still concentrating on the centre of the room. 'It took a great many attempts, and each time I risked being discovered by you or the other Councillors, but it worked in the end. Now, to the portal at hand …' All of a sudden, Isaac felt a distinct change in the air. It was as though some great force were drawing his attention to the space between Torvik and Milanda, and nothing could distract him from it. Then, just like it had in the wood, a strong gust of wind came from nowhere. The tiles on the floor were now beginning to move and swirl around like a whirlpool. Right in the middle, a spot of darkness rose up and then grew larger. The edge of the portal crackled with what looked like lightning. The portal grew and grew until it almost reached Torvik and Milanda's feet, where it stopped and they reeled backwards away from the portal. They both looked drained and out of breath.

As Isaac looked at the portal, he could tell something wasn't right. While it had stopped growing, it didn't seem to have settled at all. Lightning continued to crackle all around it and the whole thing seemed to pulsate and shimmer. It was producing a low humming noise which filled the entire chamber. A little uneasy on her feet, Milanda walked around the edge of the portal, shaking with rage.

'Well, there you have it, Torvik!' she declared, striding right up to her former colleague. 'An unstable portal! Chances are it leads directly to nowhere at all, right to the Void of Nonexistence! What possible use could you have for this?'

'I can think of one ...Madam Chair!' bellowed Torvik. In one swift movement, he swung his whole arm and struck Milanda hard. Isaac cried out, but Milanda never got the chance to shout as she lost her balance and tumbled into the portal entrance. Isaac would never forget the look of shock on her face as she disappeared into the darkness. Torvik held out his right hand again. Slowly at first and then more quickly, the portal shrank and then vanished, leaving no trace of Councillor Milanda. Indeed, there was no sign anything had happened at all. No distortion, no damage to the floor whatsoever. Isaac barely noticed Torvik approaching him until he suddenly felt a hand grip his jaw. 'I can see you were watching that, young man. Make no mistake, she is gone. She no longer exists. Unless you start reading those books in earnest, you'll end up wishing you could join her.' Torvik released his grip on Isaac's face and turned to Galvina. 'Take him back to his room and have more books brought to him.' Even as he was forced from the room, Isaac was unable to take his eyes off the centre of the room, the very spot where he had just lost his only ally.

Chapter 17

Animals in the Dark

Like most things that are done in anger and on the spur of the moment when one is fourteen, Thomas regretted leaving the others almost immediately. However, being fourteen, he was too stubborn to go back and admit he'd acted rashly. He wasn't even sure if it was possible for him to find the others again. He was walking alone, in the dark, across a plain in a direction that he could only assume was the right one. Not to mention there was every chance that Monsters of all vile descriptions were lurking either in the skies above or out in the dark around him. He had no way of knowing how far he'd come already or how far there was yet to go.

He suddenly remembered what Belactacus had told Emily about the Sand dunes. He could walk right into one and wouldn't have the slightest idea he'd done so, seeing as he'd fall asleep instantly. Despite all the risks, he decided that staying put just wasn't an option. The closest to a plan he could come up with was to keep on the move, all night if need be. He fought off the urge to sleep by concentrating on improving his imaginative powers. Thomas knew he had the potential for great power, the sudden burst of his own speed had proved that. The trouble was that had been a freak accident. He needed to be able to control his own thoughts, which is a difficult enough task for any human. So often humans think of things with no idea why, including thoughts that they consider unworthy of themselves, but they thought it all the same.

Thomas started out small, trying to imagine a stone into being right in the palm of his hand. He found that it took some time and considerable effort, but eventually he managed to think up a pebble. He actually felt it form in his hand, felt it appear from nothing. This was different to accidentally conjuring up some trees and bushes, this was something he had deliberately set about creating. As he walked, he rolled the pebble inside his palm, thinking about all the things he could create and the things he could do with enough practice. By the time he reached the city, he intended to be ready to use the full force of these powers against anything or anyone that stood in his way.

Rather than throw it away, Thomas decided to pocket the stone. If only as a keepsake. It was his intention to start trying to conjure something more useful, anything he could use as a weapon. Then there were the abilities that he had seen Emily use. He tried to fly a few times, but found he was too tired and couldn't make himself so much as hover. His primary concern, however, was what he would do when the time came to fight. Emily had frozen the wings of those harpies, so Thomas was sure he could achieve something even more effective. He was sure he'd be able to shoot lasers or balls of fire, attacks powerful enough to devastate hundreds of the Monsters. He might even be able to disintegrate them entirely, if he put his mind to it.

It was when he stopped walking for a moment to consider all this that he suddenly heard footsteps behind him. He froze, faced as he was with the prospect of having to defend himself with powers he had not yet nearly begun to master. He took a deep breath and prepared to spin round. He had conjured up shelter earlier that day without even knowing it, so hopefully now his imagination would spring to his aid once again. He turned quickly on the spot, his hands raised simply because it felt right to do so.

'Hold your fire, buckaroo!' said a voice from the darkness. It certainly didn't sound like the voice of a slobbering, blood thirsty Monster. It sounded a great deal more like a teenage girl.

'Georgie? Is that you?'

'Every bit of me,' said Georgie, getting close enough for Thomas to just about see her.

'You ...you followed me?'

'Well, not right away. I had to sneak away while Emily and Belactacus were arguing.'

'Arguing? Those two? I thought they were best buddies.'

'Not at the moment. Emily was very upset. I've never seen her like that before, and that's saying something because I sprang from her imagination. She wanted to come after you but Belactacus was going on about how dangerous it was. Then she started having a go at him for keeping you in the dark about so much. I figured I could slip away without anyone noticing and I did.'

'But ...how did you catch up with me?' asked Thomas.

'You hadn't gone all that far, you just went very, very quickly. I'll admit it freaked me out a little, you darting off like that, but I had a feeling you couldn't keep it up.'

'And just what possessed you to come after me at all?' asked Thomas, unsure of how to take Georgie's last comment.

'For one thing, you don't know your way around. I do. Sort of. A bit. Besides, you shouldn't be off on your own.'

'Oh yes, because if those Monsters find me and attack you'll be loads of help,' muttered Thomas sarcastically. He felt something hit him hard on the shoulder, causing him to cry out.

'Whereas your reflexes will certainly make you a force to be reckoned with,' said Georgie scathingly.

'Sorry,' said Thomas, rubbing his sore shoulder. 'Ok, so we go on together. The question is where do we go?'

'Well, I think we're heading in the right direction for the city. Come on, champ, let's go.' The two of them carried on walking, almost exactly in the same direction as Thomas had originally been going. Thomas kept on trying to practice imagining things but he was so tired now it had become almost impossible. They had been walking for less than an hour when Georgie insisted that they stop for a rest. Rather than argue, Thomas agreed that he'd most likely have better luck exercising his powers once he was rested. It was after they stopped, however, that Thomas noticed something.

'Georgie …are there any other forests around here? Between the valley and the forest we left?'

'No, not that I know of.'

'Then we have a problem …' said Thomas quietly as he walked a little way off to his left. Even in the darkness, he could see the vague outline of a tree. As he got closer he could see there were more. 'I don't believe this …we've managed to come back on ourselves somehow! We're back at the forest!'

'Maybe that's not such a bad thing. It's better cover for somewhere to rest.'

Thomas was about to lose his temper once again and point out that this meant they were most likely further away from the city than ever before when he heard something. A sound he'd recognise in this Realm or any other.

'Wolves …' he breathed. The howling seemed to be coming from all around them. Thomas could feel a rising panic coming up from deep inside him. He couldn't decide if he should stand his ground out in the open or retreat into the forest and use the trees as cover. Despite feeling a little more alert, he still knew he was too tired to really defend himself. The absurdity of his decision to leave the others hit him full force now. He was on the cusp of facing the very things he was so determined to eradicate and he was at a loss as to what to do.

'They sound close …' said Georgie, only just hiding the nervousness in her voice. 'Maybe we should hide in the forest.'

'Yes, get up a tree, now!' ordered Thomas. Georgie took no umbrage at being told what to do on this occasion and swiftly reached the nearest tree. She managed to jump up to the lowest branch and haul herself up. Once secure, she turned to help Thomas up, but he wasn't there. He was standing a few feet away, facing the direction the howls were coming from.

'Thomas! What the hell do you think you're trying to prove? Get up here, you idiot!' Georgie hissed, but Thomas wasn't listening. He was standing with one hand slightly raised, the other at his side. He could feel the pebble in his pocket and thought back to the first time he faced the Monsters with nothing more than a stone in his hand. Now he potentially had unlimited power, but no knowledge of how to unlock it. However, just like that first time, running didn't seem to be much of an option. These creatures were fast and could probably see in the dark much better than him or Georgie. It was time to stand.

The howls had now turned to growls, and they sounded incredibly close. Suddenly, Thomas saw something moving in the darkness only a few feet away from him. There was no denying it was a wolf, smaller than the one he had seen out in the Barren Thought Lands, but still larger than a normal wolf. It was quickly joined by another, and then another. The three wolves prowled around Thomas in a semi-circle, seemingly knowing that he wouldn't attempt to escape into the forest. Thomas was trying to muster all his creative thoughts into something he could use to attack them when the wolf directly in front of him threw its head back and let out a particularly piercing howl. Both Thomas and Georgie had to clamp their hands over their ears.

Shaking his head vigorously as the noise died down, Thomas turned his attention to the centre wolf and started to think of lasers and explosions, hoping he could shoot a quick blast at the wolf before turning to the others. Suddenly, the air in front of him seemed to distort and warp, leaving Thomas unsure if this was something he was doing or not. He became convinced of the latter when a figure materialized out of thin air. It was a Bogeyman and one that looked every inch a Bogeyman. Slime dripped from everywhere that slime could drip. The eyes were sunken and larger than normal human eyes. The Bogeyman leered, revealing sharp and broken teeth.

'Found! Found! They are found!' the disgusting creature crooned. The large eyes darted between Thomas and Georgie, who was still up in the tree. 'No …only one is human …still, one is better than none! Better! The boy! The boy will come, now!'

'I think I'll stay where I am, thanks,' said Thomas bluntly, desperately trying to decide what to attack first and perhaps just as importantly, how to attack.

'The boy can come, now! Travel with me through the shadows …quick, safe …or the boy can travel with arms in the jaws of wolves …much pain …choose, boy!' shouted the Bogeyman. Just behind him, the wolves lowered their heads and growled. Thomas knew the time to attack was now. He was going to set them on fire. He concentrated as hard as he could on the notion of heat, tried to visualise the flames shooting from his fingertips when he heard something in the distance.

For a moment Thomas thought it was another wolf or some other Monster come to join in the stand-off. This idea was shattered when a great blurred form barrelled right into the wolves and the Bogeyman. While Thomas could not see what happened next, he could certainly hear the horrendous noises. The wolves were yelping in pain and yet the Bogeyman's screams could be heard over them. A particularly loud cry from one of the wolves was cut short by a nasty crunching sound. Thomas thought he could hear the remaining wolves retreating, the sound of their pitiful whines growing more distant. It was at this point that the Bogeyman came to its senses and vanished into the darkness, leaving Thomas and

Georgie alone with the mysterious newcomer. It left what remained of the third wolf and rounded on them. Thomas knew now that he didn't have the energy or the skill to conjure anything to defend himself with. He was too tried to even keep his eyes open, so he closed them and waited for death. What he got was a whiskery sniff to the face.

Daring to open his eyes, Thomas found himself looking at a sabre tooth tiger. It wasn't snarling but there was no mistaking those enormous teeth. It just seemed curious about Thomas and had clearly decided he was not a threat. Thomas raised his hand cautiously to the tiger's head, fully aware that one bite could take off his entire arm. He could hear Georgie shouting at him, telling him not to be an idiot, but he felt anything but. As he patted the side of the tiger's face, it began to purr extraordinarily deeply. Thomas almost didn't hear the sound of more footsteps coming out of the darkness.

'Thomas! Thomas! Oh, thank the Realm Maker you're alright!' gasped Belactacus, slightly out of breath from running.

'I'm fine …we're both fine,' said Thomas quietly, still stroking the head of the enormous tiger. 'Where did this come from?'

'You can thank me for that!' came another voice. Emily was just a few paces behind Belactacus, and she in turn was closely followed by Clark. Georgie jumped down from the tree and ran to hug Emily.

'You …you imagined this tiger?' said Thomas.

'Well, yes! We heard the wolves nearby and I thought of something to protect us.'

'How did you come up with a sabre tooth tiger?'

'Well, obviously we needed something that could take on a pack of wolves, otherwise what's the point? Plus, I've always really wanted a cat, but dad is allergic.'

'Yes, it's a very impressive animal …are you sure it's tame?' asked Clark nervously.

'If Emily imagined him as a protective guardian, I doubt it will hurt anyone she considers a friend,' said Belactacus. 'Unless we are foolish enough to give it a reason.' Keeping a wary eye on the tiger, Belactacus moved closer to Thomas. 'Thomas, please accept my apologies. It was quite unfair of me to tar you with the same brush as some of your race. It is quite natural for you to be angry, given your circumstances …and at least your desire to use your imaginative power to save your brother is a noble motive. I only wished to convey to you what such unadulterated power can do to a person.'

'It's ok …I understand,' said Thomas. 'I'm sorry for going off on one like that. It turns out that I'm not as imaginative as I thought though. The only thing I've managed to think up all night was a stone. Barely a pebble, really. I couldn't think up anything when those wolves attacked. Not even when that …that thing appeared.' At this, Belactacus made Thomas describe the Bogeyman in every gruesome detail.

'If that Bogeyman escaped then he will most certainly have reported back to Torvik. Whatever we do now, we cannot stay here. Thomas, if you come with us now to the Heroes' camp, I make a solemn promise to you, here and now, that together we will devise a plan to save your brother. What do you say?' This was a first for Thomas, either in the Realm of Imagination or the Realm of Reality. He was being spoken to as an equal, or what someone younger than him might call 'a grown up'. Needless to say, it was a welcome change.

'I say lead the way!'

Chapter 18

Dealing with Rudeness

Belactacus did indeed lead the way back through the forest. They were too far from the rest of the group to rejoin them back at the makeshift camp but Belactacus assured Emily and Thomas not to worry about them. They had been well hidden and knew precisely where to go come the morning. Apparently Councillor Gumm had stopped feeling so sorry for himself and had promised to lead the surviving Friends. After getting a few hours sleep in a small clearing, Thomas and the others made their way deeper into the forest. They ate what little rations they had on the way. It wasn't long after setting off that Thomas noticed something was missing.

'Emily …where did the sabre tooth tiger go?'

'Oh, she's around. Prowling about ahead of us, I expect. Cats like to do that, even the big ones. She went off just before you got up. Oh, and her name is Tiddles.'

'Beg your pardon?' snorted Thomas.

'That's what I've decided to call her. It's irony,' said Emily very bluntly. At that precise moment, Tiddles came charging through the bushes ahead of them. She knocked Clark over as she ran, stopping just short of Emily, whom she clearly recognised as her mistress. Now that Thomas saw her in the daylight, he noticed something about her. Something altogether very distinctive.

'Emily ...she's pink!'

'And why shouldn't she be pink?' said Emily as she reached up to scratch the pre-historic pussy cat behind the ear. 'I imagined her, and I decided she should be pink.'

'Never mind what colour she is, why has she come back in such a hurry?' asked Clark as he dusted himself off. 'She seems flustered.' Tiddles was indeed breathing very heavily and seemed to be seeking comfort from Emily.

Thomas couldn't help but wonder what could possibly harass a sabre tooth tiger. Then, he heard the most peculiar sound coming from somewhere ahead of him.

'That ...that sounds like ...farting?' said Thomas incredulously. There was no mistaking it as it got louder. Great, wet raspberry noises were coming from somewhere and they seemed to be getting closer. Clark shook his head in disbelief and Belactacus closed his eyes wearily. 'What? What is it?' asked Thomas.

'Rudes,' said Belactacus irritably as all of a sudden, a dozen or so little creatures came bursting through trees and bushes all around them. They moved very quickly, and as a few of them danced and dashed around Tiddles, Thomas saw how they had been able to exasperate her. They were far too quick for her to catch and they cackled and made rude noises as her paws continued to miss them. Two more of the creatures were clutching onto Clark's legs, forcing him to kick about vigorously in an attempt to dislodge them. These were the only ones holding still long enough for Thomas to get a look at them. They looked like fat little gremlins, which made their speed all the more surprising. They were looking up at Clark with small, beady eyes and cackling through yellow teeth. Their skin was dark green and riddled with bumps and although neither Emily nor Georgie were particularly squeamish, they found themselves crying out as the Rudes danced around them and poked at them.

'Show us your knickers!' one of them screeched, causing the others to cackle even more loudly.

'Just what are these things?' shouted Thomas over the din.

'Up yours!' bellowed a Rude.

'Manifestations of all the rude and generally impolite things people in your Realm imagine themselves doing but don't,' explained Belactacus, swatting at a Rude that had swooped down close to his head. 'They're generally considered pests.'

'Pests? Pests? Pests!' screeched one of the Rudes. This set off an entire chorus with all the Rudes chanting 'Pests' over and over.

'Why not take that sword and shove it up your bum?' shouted another of the Rudes, provoking renewed and particularly shrill laughter. The noise was getting almost unbearable. Thomas could no longer hear what Belactacus was trying to tell him, but he got the general idea. If they didn't find a way to silence these creatures they were going to attract the attention of some passing Monster.

Thomas' first thought was how to destroy the Rudes but almost immediately felt ashamed. These were living things, and so far they hadn't actually done anything to harm anyone. They were just being extremely annoying, which was their nature. So instead of destroying them, he focused on finding a way merely to silence them. What happened next only took a handful of split seconds but to Thomas it happened in slow and flowing stages. Firstly, he blocked out all the noise that the Rudes were making, then he silenced his own thoughts. His mind became as tranquil and blank as it could be while he was still technically awake. Next he could feel rather than see an image forming in his mind's eye, which was now clearer than it had ever been in his life. It was a simple image of a simple object. If someone else could have seen into his mind, they would have questioned whether what they were seeing was a handkerchief or a bandage of some kind. Thomas, however, knew exactly what it was.

The final stage was clear, and he nearly laughed at how easy it now seemed. Thomas allowed his mind to open and release the image, casting it out into the space around him. To everyone else it happened all in a flash and they were quite surprised to find that every single Rude now had a gag tied around their mouths. They weren't nearly as surprised as the Rudes, of course, who made their displeasure clear by alternating between hopping up and down and making every rude gesture known. They even made a few that weren't known to anyone but them alone.

'Nicely done, Thomas,' said Belactacus genially. 'Come on, this way.' Belactacus led them further into the forest. The muffled protests of the Rudes soon died away entirely. They stayed exactly where they were in order to try and remove the gags. As he walked slightly ahead of the others, Thomas suddenly found Belactacus walking beside him. 'You could have killed them,' said the old Librarian quietly. 'I did denounce them as pests.'

'There was no need, really,' said Thomas solemnly.

'I'm very impressed, Thomas,' said Belactacus, equally as solemnly. 'There are times when one has no choice but to fight in order to defend oneself or others, but there are times when other solutions are possible. Very often it takes someone who is truly imaginative to find them.'

'If that's so, then why haven't I thought of a way to save Isaac?' asked Thomas morosely.

'We shall find one together. The fort is not far away now. It's always best to plan from a position of strength.'

They walked for the rest of the morning until they reached the foot of the mountains. Emerging from the forest, they found a vast clearing. Whereas the camp in the valley had been mostly constructed from wood, this one looked a good deal sturdier. High stone walls made up the fortress, making a semi-circle from one side of the clearing to the other, leading into the side of the mountain itself. There was only one entrance, a large iron gate right in the middle of the wall. As they got closer they could see that Heroes were patrolling along the top of the wall. Many of them stood with bows ready.

'I think, perhaps, that your feline friend should wait here at the edge of the forest, Emily,' said Belactacus. 'We don't wish to alarm anyone, especially not those who are inclined to shoot first and ask questions later, if at all.' Emily agreed, but getting Tiddles to do the same proved problematic. Emily eventually convinced her to stay. There is perhaps no stranger sight than a sabre tooth tiger looking longingly at someone as they walk away, like a kitten being left at home. They approached the gate and Belactacus called up to the Heroes on the wall, announcing his name and requesting entrance to the camp. One of the Heroes called down to someone that they couldn't see, and moments later another Hero appeared on the wall.

'Belactacus? Is that really you?' hollered the Hero.

'Verisimilitude!' answered Belactacus. While this one word made no sense to Emily, Thomas or Georgie, it seemed to mean something to the Hero standing above them. He motioned for the gates to be opened then gestured for Thomas and the others to proceed. Noticing the puzzled look on Thomas' face, Belactacus explained. 'In times such as these, people in positions such as mine have a password to prove our identity.'

'Is that really necessary?' asked Thomas.

'Very much so,' snapped Clark. Thomas was about to round on him, but Belactacus intervened.

'It has long been rumoured that some of the Monsters possess the ability to change shape. So far that's all it is, rumours …but it's best to err on the side of caution.'

'So why that particular word?' asked Emily.

'I just happen to like the sound of it,' said Belactacus casually as the gates swung open and they entered the fortress. Straight ahead of them they could see a large building made of the same stone as the wall. It looked like an enormous bunker, squat and rectangular and had obviously been built for function rather than aesthetic design. They saw horses being led across the camp towards a series of stables at the far end of the fort. All around the bunker were tents of various sizes and outside of some of these were Heroes doing the things soldiers normally do when battle is imminent. Namely sharpening weapons, making arrows and sparring with each other. Here and there were groups of refugee Friends who had escaped from the city.

As the gates closed behind them, Thomas and the others were met by a Hero, who introduced himself as Corporal Pilat.

'If you'll all come with me, I can arrange shelter for you. Belactacus, I've been asked to debrief you by Colonel Ryarn. Hopefully you can shed some light on what's been happening out there,' said Corporal Pilat, making as if to lead them all towards the huddles of refugees.

'Alternatively, Corporal, you can escort myself and these children to Colonel Ryarn immediately. We would speak with her directly,' said Belactacus pleasantly. The Corporal bristled visibly at this.

'With all due respect to your position within the Impossible City, you have no authority here, Belactacus. Now, please come with …' The good Corporal had stopped talking when he suddenly and quite unexpectedly saw that his armour had turned into candy floss. Thomas had to suppress an almighty guffaw, while Georgie was not so successful and began tittering uncontrollably. Before Corporal Pilat could say a word, Emily raised her hand.

'That was me. I did that. Now, unless you want your sword turned into a candy cane, I suggest you take us to the Colonel just like Belactacus asked.' Corporal Pilat looked from Emily to Belactacus, his expression a mixture of shock, rage and awe. Mustering himself, he inclined his head in the direction of the bunker and began marching towards it rather stiffly. Thomas surmised that the Corporal must command a great deal of respect from the other Heroes, as no one was laughing. In fact they were concentrating incredibly hard on what they were doing. He then noticed Belactacus lean in as they walked so that he could whisper to both him and Emily.

'Normally I would not approve, but you may have saved us a lot of unnecessary fuss. We need the officers in command of this camp to believe you are human, so be prepared in case any of the others need convincing.'

Upon reaching the bunker, Corporal Pilat motioned for the two Heroes guarding the door to step aside and he opened it himself. His ability to cross the camp without any of his armour falling away from him was impressive, though his face was beginning to turn red from the indignity of the whole thing. The redness of his face and the pinkness of his armour clashed a little.

'You'll forgive me if I don't come in,' said Corporal Pilat through gritted teeth. 'I'm sure you'll explain yourselves to the Colonel. Now excuse me, I need to go and change.' The door closed behind them as they entered the bunker and they heard Pilat shouting at a guard for looking at him. Georgie let out another series of titters. The bunker consisted of one large room. Dotted all around were crates of supplies and racks of weapons. Right in the middle was a long table, around which several Heroes stood. They had stopped their conversation the moment Thomas and the others had entered.

'What is this?' demanded the fair-headed Hero who stood at the head of the table. Her sharp eyes were fixed on the army's uninvited guests, particularly the children. She wore a chain mail shirt and a long skirt of the same material. It seemed clear that she was in charge, not only by her demeanour but by her position at the table. The people in charge always take up the best position at a table no matter what realm they are in. 'Belactacus? We got word you had just arrived, but I told Corporal Pilat to debrief you and report to me later! We are far too busy to …'

'I do not doubt for a moment that you are busy, Colonel,' said Belactacus, striding forward towards the table. 'However, what we have to tell you could not wait.'

150

'We?' barked Colonel Ryarn.

'Indeed. Myself and these two human children,' said Belactacus. He turned slightly and gestured for Thomas and Emily to approach. As they did, one of the Heroes at the far side of the table let out a noise that suggested both shock and irritation.

'Humans? I can hardly believe my eyes! It is you again!'

Thomas recognised the Hero who was pointing at him so directly. It was the leader of the Heroes who had saved them from the Monsters back when they first arrived, Captain Madroc. Needless to say, though we shall say it anyway, Thomas wasn't pleased at the reunion.

'Colonel, these children are no more human than you or me!' exclaimed Madroc.

'You or I,' said Emily.

'Excuse me?' snapped Madroc.

'You should have said "You or I",' said Emily calmly. 'Not "You or me".'

'Insolent and confused Friend!' snarled Madroc. He turned his attention to Thomas. 'Though if memory serves, it was you, the elder one, that gave us so much trouble last time. I see you did not get the help you so obviously need. Colonel, permission to remove these Friends from the bunker so that we can get back to …aaarrgghh!' The Captain had let out this cry, as most would in his situation, because sand had suddenly begun to pour down on his head from out of nowhere. Just regular sand, not the kind with sleep-inducing properties. It fell quickly and in great amounts, and within seconds had not only pooled at the bottom of his feet but had swiftly piled up to his knees. As it began to reach his middle, Belactacus turned to Thomas.

'I think the good Captain is quite convinced now, Thomas.' Unable to stop himself grinning, Thomas stopped the sand. It had taken a bit of concentration on his part to make it happen, but the idea had come into his head quite naturally. Captain Madroc was too busy kicking sand away to protest further, so Belactacus took the opportunity to address the gathered officers. 'Ladies and gentlemen, you're all fully aware of what humans in our Realm would be capable of. You have just seen it for yourself. So I think any further debate as to whether or not these children have the right to be heard would be pointless.'

'So you brought them here to threaten us?' shouted the Hero on Madroc's right.

'Not at all,' said Belactacus, calmly as ever.

'We're going to help,' said Thomas, speaking up for the first time since entering the bunker. He ignored the glare from Captain Madroc and stepped closer to the table. 'My brother is being held captive in the city, and I'm going to get him out. He's being held by Torvik. He's in charge of the Monsters.'

At this news, the assembled officers all looked at each other uncertainly.

'Councillor Torvik was behind the attack?' said Colonel Ryarn. 'I find it hard to believe that a Councillor would ally themselves with the Monsters ...'

'He has not only allied himself with them, he is their leader,' said Belactacus, now speaking in a much more serious tone. 'He has organised them to a degree we have never seen before and indeed never thought possible. We have heard this from another Councillor, Councillor Gumm.'

'Where is he?' asked Colonel Ryarn.

'In the forest. He should be on his way, along with a number of other survivors from the city. Has there been any word from any of the other Councillors?'

'None,' said Colonel Ryarn. 'We're sure that Councillor Callion would make his way here in an emergency. However, we know he was in the city at the time of the attack. He had reported back there for an emergency session of the Council a few days ago.'

'That explains why Torvik was so eager to arrange the emergency session in the first place,' said Clark, unaware at first that all eyes in the room were now on him. 'He must have wanted to assemble the Council in one place before launching the attack.'

'Indeed, Clark,' said Belactacus. 'We know that Gumm escaped, and as well as Callion, Councillors Clou and Milanda are unaccounted for.'

'We cannot afford to wait for them,' declared a brash young Hero. 'For every minute we wait, the Monsters' position within the City becomes stronger. We must attack now!'

'Our numbers are too few,' said Colonel Ryarn bitterly. 'When the Monsters were disorganised we could out manoeuvre them and pick them off a few at a time, keeping them at bay. Now that they are united under their new leader we cannot hope to match their forces.'

It was then that Thomas was struck by what is commonly known as inspiration.

'What if we just took out Torvik?' he asked. All the Heroes turned to look at him, as did Belactacus. Thomas could see the concern in the older man's face but ignored it, confident that what he was about to say would allay all the fears Belactacus had confessed to having. 'If we could sneak into the city and capture Torvik, we might be able to convince him to order the Monsters to retreat. Then they'd go back to being a disorganised rabble.'

'Boy, do you have any …I mean, young man,' said Captain Madroc, seeing the looks on the faces of Thomas, Emily and Georgie. 'What you are suggesting would be extremely difficult. To enter the city at all would be hard enough, but to get through to the Tower of Realms undetected? Just how do you imagine us doing this?'

'That's just it, Captain,' said Thomas. 'We use our imaginations. Emily and I. We can use our powers to get ourselves and a small team of others into the city. If we're careful enough, we can get to Torvik undetected.'

'Wait a moment,' said a Hero standing next to the Colonel. 'Why could you not use this great power of yours to aid us in our fight? Why, you could wipe out the Monsters with a single thought! Victory could be ours in a matter of moments!' Belactacus bristled visibly at this, and was about to speak when Thomas beat him to it.

'No, absolutely not.'

'Ah, I see,' said Captain Madroc, smirking almost indecently. 'I should have known. You are a coward.'

'I stood up to you easily enough,' retorted Thomas. 'I'm not saying for a moment that I won't go up against those Monsters. There'll be plenty of them in the city, but Emily and I can use our powers to distract and confuse them while we make our way to the tower. I will not use whatever power I have to destroy.'

'Me neither,' said Emily. 'Besides, what happens if we can't control it? One wrong thought and we could wipe out your entire Realm. None of you thought of that, did you?' Several of the Heroes looked at their feet, understandably embarrassed at being lectured by a nine-year-old.

After talking at great length, it was decided that in order to make their passage through the city easier, the army would try to draw the Monsters out into battle. The quicker Thomas and Emily could get to Torvik the quicker they could force him to disperse his foul forces. Naturally they would not go alone. Belactacus would accompany them along with Captain Madroc and two of his finest fighters. Georgie had wanted to accompany them but Belactacus forbade it. Clark didn't want to go but Belactacus insisted.

'Then it is settled,' said Colonel Ryarn. 'At first light we march out to the plains in order to draw out the enemy. Captain Madroc and the others will ride out through the valley. For now, I suggest we all get some rest …and can we please find someone to sweep up all this sand?'

154

Chapter 19

Return to the Impossible City

Sleep did not come easily to anyone that night, and even if it had, they did not have long to sleep. The Heroes were up several hours before dawn, donning armour and sharpening weapons. Every horse in the stable was being dressed for battle. Thomas had spent the night in a tent with Clark and Belactacus while Georgie and Emily had a tent of their own. It was Belactacus who rose first and went to wake Thomas and Clark. They ate their breakfast, which was better than anything they had eaten since escaping the Impossible City, in relative silence. Once they were finished, they made their way to the stables, where Captain Madroc was waiting for them.

'Ah, how good of you to join us!' barked the Captain. 'My men and I are ready to go …when you are.'

'Tell me, Captain,' said Thomas dangerously. 'How would you like to be a duck?' Captain Madroc grimaced, caught between the desire to reprimand Thomas and his distaste at being so genuinely afraid of a teenager. The other Heroes assigned to join them couldn't help but snigger a little.

'Jorrar, Lancast! Fetch the steeds for our …honoured guests,' ordered Madroc. The two Heroes saluted and went into the stables. The smell of horse was strong, and it wasn't something Thomas was used to. It must have shown on Thomas' face because Madroc was smirking. 'Have you ever ridden a horse before?'

'I ...well, I ...'

'He rode a donkey once at Weston-Super-Mare,' said a voice from behind Thomas. He turned around and saw that it was Emily and she wasn't alone. 'It doesn't matter though, because we won't be using a horse.' Captain Madroc was about to ask just what they would be riding when he saw for himself just what Emily meant. Everyone around the stables noticed Tiddles striding along beside Emily, wearing what looked like a saddle on her back. The sabre toothed tiger had been made to sleep outside the gates during the night, but Emily had risen especially early and gone to fetch her. If the Heroes weren't wary of her after the whole candy floss incident, the fact that she had a sabre tooth tiger at her command made sure they were.

Tiddles recognised Thomas and instantly went to him, purring loudly and offering the back of her head for some fuss and attention.

'Emily ...are you suggesting we ride a tiger?' asked Thomas as he obliged Tiddles by scratching her behind her ear.

'Certainly. They didn't have any saddles that fit her, so I thought one up! She can carry both of us and I bet she's faster than any horse.'

'We shall see about that, Miss,' said Madroc stiffly as his men returned with the horses. 'These fine beasts are among the fastest in the army. We shall have to ride without stopping until we reach the outskirts of the city, from there we shall have to go on foot if we wish to avoid being detected. We shall ride south, out of the forest and down to the valley. The army will be marching west in an attempt to catch the enemy's attention. We must move swiftly and accomplish our goal, or our comrades will most surely be overwhelmed. Is that understood?'

'Very clearly, Captain,' said Belactacus as he heaved himself onto his own horse. Clark was struggling to do the same when Georgie suddenly appeared from around the corner of the stable. She came and hugged Emily and for a moment it looked as though she wanted to hug Thomas too but thought better of it at the last moment. Thomas climbed into the saddle on Tiddles then Emily sat behind him. They both nearly lost their balance when Tiddles rose up. Thomas was too preoccupied with trying not to fall off to notice that Georgie was right at their side again.

'Listen,' she said somewhat shyly. 'Just …you know, both of you …do me a favour and …don't get yourselves killed, ok? Especially …' She turned a stark shade of red and looked down at her feet. Madroc gave the order to move out before Thomas could say anything and Tiddles strode away with the other horses.

'She likes you,' said Emily as they approached the gate.

'Who, Georgie? What makes you so sure?' asked Thomas.

'What makes you so unsure?' countered Emily annoyingly.

As they rode out through the gate, they found themselves alongside the rest of the army. The Heroes must have come from many different cultures all around the Realm of Reality. Thomas had never seen such a motley collection of soldiers, all armed with different weapons and dressed in different clothes, yet they all shared the same sense of discipline and timing as they marched. Most of them were on foot, though here and there were columns of cavalry. The plan was to march out and meet the Monsters head on, out on the vast plains that surrounded the Impossible City. They must have numbered in the many hundreds, but Thomas couldn't help but wonder, as they rode past on Tiddles, just how many would survive the coming battle being fought for his benefit.

Following Madroc, they rode out away from the rest of the army and turned south into the forest. They could not pick up much speed as they made their way through the forest itself, and had not been riding long when Clark let out a strangled cry.

'What? What is it?' hissed Madroc, bringing his horse to a halt. Clark pointed a shaking finger towards some distant trees. They had reached a slight hill in the forest and could still see the army snaking its way through further north, but it was something else that had caught Clark's eye.

'Down there …in the shadows of those trees …I could have sworn I saw one,' said Clark.

'Saw what?' demanded Madroc impatiently.

'Bogeyman,' said Belactacus grimly. 'It must have been watching from the shadows for any sign of movement from the fortress. It will no doubt report back to Torvik that the army is on the move. We can only hope that it did not spot us.'

'Come,' said Madroc. 'We must get out of the forest. Then we can show you just how fast these horses are!'

It turned out Tiddles was more than capable of keeping up with Madroc's horses. The plain seemed more lifeless than before as well as much colder. The dread of impending battle was thick in the air and it was as though the animals were aware of it. After they had been riding for a few hours, Thomas was beginning to feel sore in places he'd rather not mention. After riding back through the valley, they came up and out to stop on a hill that overlooked much of the city. Stopping his horse next to Tiddles, Belactacus pointed out a street in the distance.

'That is where we can enter the city. It's our best chance of getting in unseen. Leave the horses here and then …' He stopped when he saw what was happening further off towards the north. It was hardly something they could have failed to notice. A vast mass of raucous Monsters was streaming out of the city. Giant creatures could be clearly seen among the smaller ones while all around them flying Monsters flew on with terrible purpose. Some of the larger Monsters were stepping on the smaller ones, crushing them underfoot like insects. Such was their determination and single-mindedness in reaching their enemy. It was an unending horde on the ground and a massive swarm in the sky, disappearing into the distant plains.

'Thomas …look up there!' breathed Emily. Thomas' attention had momentarily been on the Monsters on the ground, but now that he looked up at the sky he saw great plumes of flame amongst the flying Monsters.

'Dragons!' gasped Clark, looking profoundly terrified.

'Our timing could not have been better,' said Madroc. 'Come, we dismount here and enter the city on foot, then …'

'There are thousands of them …' said Thomas. 'How are the others supposed to fight them?'

'My comrades are experienced warriors,' said Madroc tersely. 'They will hold out long enough for us to complete our task, but only if we make haste! Come!'

Without another word, they all dismounted. There was nowhere to latch up the horses, so they had to be set free lest they be seen by the enemy. Getting Tiddles to run free was not so easy.

'We cannot infiltrate the city with such a large beast in tow!' exclaimed Madroc. 'She will alert the enemy to our presence!'

'She won't leave me and go off on her own!' protested Emily. It took some persuasion but they managed to get Tiddles to stay where she was. They made their way down the hill to the outskirts of the city, moving quietly through the first few streets. All hopes that this part of the city was not being guarded were soon dashed. An enormous wasp, flying up and down the street as though patrolling it. The buzzing noise it was making was so loud that it drowned out anything that they tried to say to each other as they hid behind a pile of debris. Madroc began making complicated gestures to Jorarr and Lancast. Thomas had seen enough war movies to know he was giving them instructions as to how to take out the wasp. Thomas merely looked at Emily, who nodded immediately and climbed up the pile of debris. This caused Madroc to panic as he tried to scramble up and stop her. Seconds later, however, the buzzing had stopped. An uneasy silence fell over them all. Thomas, Belactacus, Clark and the Heroes all climbed up the debris to join Emily, where they saw that the wasp was trapped inside a giant jar. It had been sealed tight, rendering the wasp silent, extremely annoyed but essentially harmless.

'I think, Captain, that you've forgotten why Thomas and I came along,' said Emily smugly as she climbed over the top of the wreckage and started climbing down the other side. Looking suitably embarrassed, Madroc climbed up after her, followed closely by the others.

As they made their way through the rest of the city, they came across other solitary Monsters patrolling the streets. On each occasion they were able to distract or incapacitate the Monster using the power of Emily and Thomas' creative thoughts. Often enough it was a simple matter of thinking up a strange sound in the distance and moving swiftly on when the Monster went to investigate. On one or two occasions they had to imagine various ways of trapping them, including ropes and gags like Thomas had used on the Rudes. Emily had become quite adept at conjuring more of the giant jars. Belactacus would later comment that every person had their own special talents when it came to creative thought, assuming of course that they weren't Un. In just over an hour they had come to the city's main square, on the other side of which stood the Tower of Realms. Unfortunately, dashing across the square was not an option.

'What's happening?' asked Clark, as he was roughly pressed against the wall of a building by Lancast. Madroc was peering round the corner, a grim frown on his face.

'Monsters. Far too many of them and …there are Friends.'

'What?' said Emily, who joined Madroc at the corner in order to see for herself. She saw that the square was being used as a makeshift concentration camp, with a great number of Friends all huddled together. All around the assembled Friends, lining the edge of the square, were Monsters. Some were standing still, some were patrolling, stopping only to leer at the terrified Friends. Madroc was certainly right in that there were too many to take on.

'Is there a way around?' asked Thomas.

'Yes,' said Belactacus. 'We shall have to go back on ourselves slightly and take a left, going through the streets and then …

'Wait! What about those poor Friends? We're not just going to leave them there?' said Emily.

Everyone fell silent for a moment. Thomas did see her point. Those Friends must have been gathered there for a reason and it couldn't be good. Working together, he and Emily might be able to take on the Monsters but they were guarding the Friends so closely there was a very good chance that they could get hurt. Madroc looked on the edge of an angry retort at Emily, but Belactacus spoke first.

'Emily, there are simply too many of them. Besides, our goal is to find Torvik. If we can capture him, we can force him to order the Monsters to stand down. The army is counting on us to get to him quickly. We cannot allow ourselves to be delayed for any reason.' Emily looked uncertain, but nodded. Madroc took the lead now as they went back, then circled around through the streets. Just a few minutes later they found themselves looking out on the walls and the gateway that led to the Tower of Realms. Clark took a few steps out towards the gateway but was grabbed roughly from behind by Madroc.

'Hold a moment. Something is not right here.'

'Indeed,' said Belactacus as he surveyed their surroundings. 'There isn't a Monster in sight. Not one.'

'But why put so many Monsters out in the city square and yet leave the main entrance to the tower unguarded?' ventured Lancast.

'It's a trap,' said Thomas. 'It's very obviously a trap. Torvik must know we're coming.'

'Very possible,' said Belactacus.

'Do we call it off?' asked Clark timidly.

'There is a great deal at stake,' said Belactacus. 'However, as the two most powerful members of our little task force, it should be Thomas and Emily who make the final decision. What do you think?'

Thomas and Emily looked at each other for all of a few seconds. The look on Emily's face said it all. She intended to see this through to the end. Thomas felt very much the same.

'We go on,' he said simply.

'Indeed we shall!' said Belactacus fervently. 'Torvik could be anywhere in the tower, so we should split up to search for him. Emily, you go with Clark, Lancast and Jorarr. Thomas, you come with Madroc and myself. Now, onwards!' Unsheathing his own sword, Belactacus now led them all as they ran towards the gateway. There were no Monsters in the courtyard waiting for them so they crossed entirely unopposed. The same went for their entry to the main building at the base of the tower, and even the reception was deserted. They stopped for a moment to look around. The silence was on the verge of being the disquieting, overwhelming sort but ultimately it didn't last long enough to be so. Not five seconds after they had entered the building, it started to shake. An almighty roar came from somewhere above them, followed by a deep humming that resonated from every wall.

'What is that?' shouted Madroc.

'Trouble,' said Belactacus. He pointed his sword towards the staircase at the far end of the reception. 'Those stairs lead up to the separate sides of the tower. Thomas, Madroc and I will go to the left. Everyone else, the right!' As the group ran towards the stairs and split, Emily and Thomas exchanged one last look before the stairs forced them to turn away. Now Thomas had only Belactacus and Madroc for company as they searched every corridor and room for Torvik. All hostility he once felt or indeed continued to feel towards these two disappeared out of necessity, replaced with only a single drive to find his brother.

The humming sound became louder as they went upwards, searching each corridor and then taking the next flight of stairs to the level above them. Each room and chamber they searched was empty. They were beginning not only to fret as they reached the tenth floor but also to run out of breath. Just as they reached the next staircase they heard someone cry out nearby. Very nearby indeed. Nearby enough to have come from the floor above them. Without a word they tore up the stairs and burst through the doors to the eleventh floor. Unlike all those beneath them, this floor was not a single corridor but rather a whole room. Columns supported the ceiling and further on from where Thomas now stood, to his right, a set of steps led downwards. It was here that the humming sound was strongest. Directly across from the door stood Torvik, his sword sheathed and the scruff of Isaac's shirt held tightly in his hand.

Chapter 20

The Final Attempt

'You'd be well advised to stop right where you are, all of you!' declared Torvik as soon as they had all entered the room. Belactacus and Madroc both still had their swords drawn but did indeed stop when they saw the hold that Torvik had on Isaac, who was looking distinctly tired but generally unharmed. Thomas stopped too, but kept his eyes firmly fixed on Torvik.

'Isaac, are you alright?' he asked.

'He's more than alright, aren't you Isaac?' said Torvik most casually. 'He's been my guest.'

'Strange. He looks more like a prisoner to me,' said Madroc dangerously.

'Call him what you like, the point is he has not been harmed …recently,' retorted Torvik, not nearly as casually as before. 'Kindly take a moment, gentlemen, to take stock of your situation. First of all, take a look over the rail …go on …I insist.' Torvik indicated the rail that separated the raised platform from the floor below. He was standing very close to it, with Isaac held even closer. Belactacus, Thomas and Madroc edged just close enough to be able to see over the rail, and whether they recognised it or not, what they saw shocked them all. All that could be seen at the foot of the steps was a mass of darkness, while the last few steps themselves looked distorted and warped. A large, unstable portal covered the whole floor. They quickly edged away at the sight of it. Madroc in particular was visibly shaken.

'That's …that's …'

'Entirely unstable, yes,' said Torvik, 'I do have high hopes of making it stable though, with a little help. Now, how about we say hello to my friend over there?' Torvik now indicated the corner of the room with his free hand, and there in the shadows to his right, stood a Bogeyman with the most obscene smile imaginable on his face. 'Now, should anyone try anything too sudden, our Bogeyman friend will instantly disappear and reappear in the square below. Once he does he will give the order for the immediate execution of every Friend the Monsters are guarding.'

'I had a feeling that was why they were being held down there,' said Belactacus, unable to hide the disgust in his tone. 'I did not think you capable of such cowardice.'

'I see it more as an insurance policy,' said Torvik. 'Here's my other guarantee that you'll listen.' At this he jostled Isaac slightly but visibly. Isaac didn't resist and Thomas had a feeling that this was because his brother didn't have the strength. 'Make no mistake, I have no qualms about tossing my young guest here over the rail. So even if you managed to stop my Bogeyman, you could never rescue the boy in time.'

'You foul, despicable wretch!' bawled Madroc. 'A traitor to us all!'

'If all you're going to do is insult me, Captain, then you can leave. Run along and see if you can find Emily for me,' said Torvik. When Madroc did not move, Torvik jostled Isaac again, pushing him a little closer to the rail. 'Now, Captain!' Madroc quickly looked to Belactacus and then to Thomas, who nodded just ever so slightly. Keeping his sword in his hand, Madroc backed out of the room and left. Thomas edged closer to Belactacus.

'Belactacus …what would happen to Isaac if he fell into that thing?'

'I'm afraid I don't know for certain. If it is even remotely stable, he may come out in your world, the Realm of Reality …but there's no way of knowing where he may come out. A country far away from your home … the middle of a desert or an ocean.'

'What if it's not stable?'

'Then he will fall into the Void and be trapped there. With no opening to the Realm of Reality he would …cease to exist.'

'I could not have put it better myself, Belactacus,' said Torvik. 'Then again, you always were good with words. Must be all the books.'

'Words are indeed useful to have at my disposal, but you'll find me more than ready to act, should the occasion arise,' said Belactacus, tightening his grip on the hilt of his sword. 'You have our full attention, Torvik.'

'I do, don't I? The fact is, Thomas, I need your help.'

'My …my help?' said Thomas, unable to believe his own ears.

'I need you to help me stabilise the portal to your Realm. The power of your imagination can do that. It pains me to have to resort to measures such as holding your brother and those Friends hostage, but it was the only way to ensure you'd hear me out. Once the portal is stable, I and anyone else who chooses to follow me can leave this Realm and enter yours. We can become Real. That's all I have ever wanted, Thomas, but the Council has always strictly controlled what can become Real and what cannot. They are and always have been unwilling to listen to reason. All I ask is the chance to decide my own destiny. There are Friends who feel the same way I do and once the portal is stabilised, they can come with me and truly live their own lives …not have their very existence tied to someone else. Help me bring that about and your family can come with us! What do you say, Thomas?'

All of this caught Thomas by surprise. Everything he had heard since the Monsters attacked the city had led him to believe that Torvik was the villain behind it all. Yet, as he spoke, he sounded so sincere. Was it possible that all this had been a misunderstanding or that Thomas had actually been lied to by the others? Belactacus, Clark and Gumm, could they all have got it wrong? Thomas could feel doubt sitting in his mind like someone might sit precariously on a wall. Sure enough though, something else came along to push doubt off the wall. It's sometimes called intuition, or else a gut feeling. He couldn't say what, but there was something about Torvik that made it very hard to trust him anymore. He didn't realise it at the time, but it was the sight of Isaac and the distressed state Torvik had so clearly left him in.

'I don't believe you,' said Thomas bluntly. Torvik's expression changed in an instant. It was as though the words from Thomas' mouth had slammed a door shut. 'It was so easy to trust you when we first met …but now there's something different …'

'There certainly is,' said Belactacus, stepping closer to Thomas. 'His powers are weaker from opening up the portal. You're not a Friend, are you Torvik? You've led everyone to believe you are, but you're something else entirely. You're a manifestation.'

'Very clever, Belactacus,' said Torvik. 'Yes, I am like you and yet so much greater. I am the collected creative thoughts of all those who plot and scheme. Backstabbers and conspirators created me, from the assassins of Julius Caesar and Caligula to the modern day political takeovers! I am treachery and deceit in humanoid form, a form it took many centuries to take, but as humanity become more creative and covert in their underhanded ways, I became stronger!'

'That also explains how you marshalled the Monsters,' said Belactacus. 'They'd never listen to just anyone …but they would follow one of their own.'

'Ouch, a little below the belt, don't you think?' laughed Torvik mockingly. 'Still, it doesn't matter that young Thomas here won't see sense. Willing or not, I shall harness your imaginative powers and use them to boost my own power. My army will swarm into your Realm and take it by force. We shall master our own destiny by becoming the masters of humanity!'

'You'll have to get to me first!' hollered Thomas over the sound of the portal, which now seemed to be getting louder. Out of the corner of his eye, he noticed that the Bogeyman appeared nervous, wringing its hands and glancing between Torvik and Thomas. Then suddenly, a tremor resonated throughout the building, travelling across the very floor they stood on. Thomas felt it pulsate through his body for the briefest of moments.

'The portal is becoming even more unstable!' shouted Belactacus, 'Torvik, if it is not closed now we may all be pulled in! Our entire Realm will be destroyed!'

'It will be destroyed anyway, once I find and kill the Caretaker!' declared Torvik. 'Hand the boy over to me, Belactacus, and I can stabilise it! I promise he will not be harmed!'

'Save your lies! I know that what you hope to do would devastate Thomas' mind and leave him with nothing, not even his own thoughts! Release Isaac, now!'

'Certainly!' exclaimed Torvik, who proceeded to not just release Isaac, but launch him over the rail. Thomas didn't cry out, nor did he rush to the rail, because he knew he did not have the time to do either. Instead, almost instinctually, he sought to use his power. He found himself imagining how easy it would be to save his brother if only he had the ability to levitate objects with his mind, the power known as telekinesis. Immediately he could feel this ability come to him. It felt wonderful and new, yet at the same time strangely familiar. He reached out with his mind, as though his very thoughts now had arms, hands and fingers. He grabbed hold of Isaac, who came to a firm halt in mid-air, suspended over a chasm of sheer and literal nothingness.

Taking hold of Isaac had proved to be easy, but holding on to him turned out to be more difficult. Thomas became only vaguely aware of what was going on around him as he found he had to concentrate harder and harder just to stop Isaac from falling. He could feel the pull of the portal working against him, trying to wrench Isaac from his telekinetic grasp. He slowly walked closer to the rail so that he could now actually see his brother, spread-eagled in the air. He could hear the sound of blades clashing violently and assumed that Belactacus and Torvik were duelling. He thought he heard the door burst open but it was all just background noise to Thomas, who was trying with all his mental might to pull Isaac to safety.

As the portal became more unstable, the pull became stronger. Thomas' whole body tensed as he focused every fibre of his being on his task, though at the back of his mind he knew he could not hold Isaac forever. His grip weakened for a moment and Isaac inched closer to the portal. Thomas quickly redoubled his efforts when suddenly he heard a cry from somewhere behind him. He turned his head ever so slightly and in the corner of his eye he could see Torvik. He had his sword raised high, ready to strike as he advanced on Thomas, a calm and cruel look on his face. Thomas knew that if he tried to defend himself he would lose his grip on Isaac, yet if he did nothing they were both doomed. Just at the moment when he knew Torvik's attack must be imminent, he saw something barrel into Torvik, tackling him. Torvik and his attacker both hit the rail with great force and went tumbling over the side. It was then that Thomas recognised his mysterious saviour. It was Clark!

Though close to exhaustion, Thomas used his newfound ability and reached out with his mind once again, grabbing hold of Clark and holding onto him. Both Clark and Isaac were suspended mere feet from each other, but unfortunately they were not alone. Torvik had managed to grab hold of Isaac's arm and was gripping tight, causing Isaac a great deal of pain. What's more, Thomas could feel his grip on Isaac slipping. He could feel as well as see Torvik writhing in the air, hanging from Isaac's arm. Torvik's face was contorted, but it was impossible to tell if it was fear or hatred that distorted his handsome features. He seemed to be trying to pull himself up and grab hold of Isaac with his other hand, but Isaac had other ideas. Weakened though he was from his captivity, he had one course of action left to him despite not having done it since he was a toddler. He thrust his head towards Torvik's hand and sank his teeth in, biting down hard. Nobody heard Torvik's agonised cry over the sound of the portal, but they saw him falling. There being absolutely nothing to land on, he simply disappeared. Even without Torvik struggling and pulling at Isaac, Thomas was still having trouble holding both him and Clark.

For a moment, the grim thought crossed his mind that if he allowed one to drop he might be able to save the other. He wanted nothing more than to save his brother, but Clark had saved his life only moments ago. He had no time to ponder the decision, so he didn't. He chose not to doom one to save the other. He would use his power to save them both or die trying. All around him he could hear people shouting, but the voices were muffled and vague. He thought he felt a hand on his shoulder but his whole body was too numb to really register it. All that mattered was keeping Isaac and Clark from harm, but that soon became too great a task. As his last ounce of concentration left him, he felt them both slip from his grip entirely. He would have cried out but he no longer had the strength. All sensation left him and he slipped into unconsciousness, just as surely as though he had been hit in the face with a bucketful of Sand.

Chapter 21

When All is Well

The first thing Thomas noticed when he came around was how quiet everything was. There was no humming noise at all now. When he opened his eyes, he saw Georgie's face directly above him.

'Hey, Tommy Tom Tom, how are you feeling?' she asked softly.

'Bad enough, thanks,' replied Thomas hoarsely. With some help from Georgie, he was able to sit up. Looking round he saw that he was still in the Tower of Realms, right by the rail. A sudden panic gripped him as he remembered what had happened and he tried to get up altogether too quickly.

'Relax, relax!' insisted Georgie. 'Everything's okay!'

'But Isaac …and Clark …they …'

'Are a little winded from hitting the floor, but otherwise we're quite well,' said a nearby voice. Thomas looked to his left and saw Clark and Isaac, the latter of whom dropped down on his knees to Thomas' side.

'Thank you …thank you, Thomas,' said Isaac quietly. He leant forward to give his brother the closest thing to a hug he'd given him in many years. Whereas a few days ago Thomas might have pushed him off, now he gently squeezed Isaac's shoulder. Across the room he could see Emily kneeling next to Belactacus along with a Hero that Thomas didn't recognise.

'What happened?' asked Thomas. 'Is Belactacus …'

'He's ok,' said Georgie. 'Well, he will be. Torvik didn't wound him that badly and Galvus over there is a pretty good medic.'

'Galvus? Who's Galvus? How did he …or come to think of it, how did you get here?' asked Thomas, looking directly at Georgie.

'Councillor Callion brought me. Not long after you and the rest of the army left, he turned up at the camp. Turns out he'd been off gathering up all the patrols that were scattered about all over the place. I told him about what you were all off to do and …'

'He brought you with him?' spluttered Thomas. 'To a city crawling with Monsters?'

'I didn't give him much of a choice,' said Georgie slyly. 'See, before I told him what you were up to, I made him swear to take me with him. Heroes tend to keep their word and all that.'

Unable to believe his ears, Thomas tried to think of words to express his surprise but none could be found in his exhausted brain. He was quite grateful, therefore, when Emily came over to them.

'You're awake!' she exclaimed. 'How are you feeling?'

'A little worse for wear, but I'll be alright. Would someone mind telling me what happened …in general? Things got a little fuzzy for a while …'

'Emily and I were searching rooms on the other side of the tower when we came across Captain Madroc who told us what was happening in here,' said Clark. 'Emily ran off to the room and I ran after her. When I got here, Belactacus and Torvik were fighting and Emily had a Bogeyman well and truly cornered.'

'Cornered? How?' asked Thomas. Emily suddenly adopted her usual look of being far too pleased with herself.

'I imagined a ray of sunlight right onto the Bogeyman. They hate daylight, so he couldn't move. I was concentrating so hard on keeping the Bogeyman from disappearing that by the time I saw that Belactacus was hurt it was too late.'

'That's where I, quite literally, came in,' said Clark.

'You saved my life, thank you, Clark,' said Thomas. 'Who closed the portal?'

'I did,' said Emily. 'After Clark tackled Torvik I could tell you were having trouble so I had to leave the Bogeyman and go to help you. Belactacus told me to just imagine myself closing the portal. It wasn't easy but I managed it, just before Clark and Isaac fell. The Bogeyman got away.'

'The Friends!' exclaimed Thomas. 'Down in the square!'

'Calm down, young man. They have not been harmed,' said the voice of Captain Madroc. It seemed he had been consulting with some other Heroes down the stairs where the portal had been and had only now just come up. 'It seems the Bogeyman panicked when he saw Torvik defeated and far from ordering the Monsters to attack, he told them to retreat. The Monsters were thrown into disarray, and even now Councillor Callion is leading our forces in an effort to make sure they are driven right back to the Barren Thought Lands. I heard how you stood up to Torvik, Thomas. A true Hero can admit when he is wrong, and I have misjudged you. Please, let me shake you by the hand and consider you a friend, if you'll pardon the expression.'

Thomas happily took the captain's outstretched hand and shook it, then was helped to stand upright by Madroc and the others. With help from Georgie, he walked over to where Belactacus was being helped onto a stretcher by two Heroes. Thomas could see that a dressing had been applied to a wound in Belactacus' right side, just above his hip. The old man smiled as he saw Thomas and Georgie approach and motioned for the two Heroes to wait a moment.

'Thomas …you did it …you and your cousin truly are the best of humanity …'

'Well, it's like you said, Belactacus …I could either have destroyed Torvik the moment we got in or …rise above him and find another way.' Belactacus smiled again and raised his hand, which Thomas took in his own and squeezed gently. The Heroes then carefully carried Belactacus away, but Thomas and the others saw him again soon enough when they all found themselves escorted down to the reception hall, which had been converted into a temporary infirmary. The army's field medics checked them over, along with a number of Heroes and Friends who had been caught up in the fighting. Thomas spent most of the day recovering, as did Isaac. The following day, he and Emily went round the city using their power wherever they could to help rebuild and undo the damage done by the Monsters. Although unable to imagine anything into being or repair anything with his mind, Isaac helped to distribute food to the citizens as they returned to the city. Thomas was naturally the first to notice the great change that had taken place in Isaac. He got the feeling that Isaac didn't want to discuss what he had been through and didn't press him, but he knew he'd be there for him if his brother ever changed his mind.

Within a few days, much of the city had been restored. Belactacus was soon well enough to return to the Library which required a great deal of reorganising after the Monsters had been rampaging through it. It was a task that he, Clark and the rest of the staff at the Library were more than capable of handling. There had been no sign of Galvina in the city and regular reports coming in from the Heroes pursuing the Monsters, gave no news of Torvik's chief aide. Her absence weighed heavily on Thomas' mind, but even more so on Isaac's. On more than one occasion he had frantically claimed to have seen her face among the crowds of busy Friends, but whenever anyone else looked she was nowhere to be seen. After this had happened for a third time, Thomas went looking for Belactacus. He found him in his private study in the

Library, sorting out his own collection of books. This time, he made sure to knock first.

'Come in, Thomas,' said Belactacus as he picked up another of his books, only to find that most of the pages had been torn out by one of the Monsters. 'Look at that, quite ruined,' he sighed. 'How any living creature can bring themselves to destroy a book I shall never know. What can I do for you, Thomas?'

'Well, it's about Galvina. Isaac said he saw her again this morning, but nobody can find her.'

'Your brother underwent a terrible ordeal at the hands of Torvik and that dreadful woman. It may take some time for him to recover.' Belactacus reached for another book but it slipped from his hand and fell to the floor. He went to pick it up but suddenly winced. Thomas quickly picked up the book for him.

'Are …are you okay, Belactacus?' he asked.

'A little sore, perhaps. It seems your brother is not the only one who will need some time to recover after having dealings with Torvik …but he and I both have people around us …people who care about us. We'll both be fine, in the end.' Thomas stayed to help Belactacus. After a few minutes, he felt compelled to ask something.

'Belactacus …about Torvik …'

'What about him?' asked Belactacus lightly.

'He said he was like you …you know …'

'We are both manifestations, yes, though of course he kept that hidden from us all.'

'So …if no one person Imagined you , does that mean that you and Sylvia can never die, the way the Friends do?' Belactacus paused at this. He gently placed the book in his hand on the shelf, then turned his gaze to the floor.

'That is quite a question from one so young. Manifestations depend on the collective consciousness of humanity, so it is true that my life force is not tied to any one person. Does this make me, Sylvia or even Torvik immortal? No. We can be hurt and destroyed easily enough.'

'Then Torvik is definitely gone? He's ceased to exist?' asked Thomas.

'That manifestation of treachery and deceit is gone, yes,' said Belactacus, looking up at Thomas so as to reassure him. 'Torvik is gone, but as long as there is treachery in the minds of human kind, a new manifestation can always arise. Do not worry, Thomas. Torvik said it took many years for him to become strong enough to take his humanoid form. I myself did not spring up overnight.'

'But you have been around a long time, haven't you?' asked Thomas, now more out of curiosity than anything else. 'Long enough to read all these books and certainly long enough to learn how to use a sword.'

'Yes, indeed. I have lived in my present form for many hundreds of years. I have seen many Friends here at the Library come and go. There was a time when I could no longer bear to lose those closest to me, especially as I knew I must linger on. So I shut myself away with my books and took up sword fighting in case the time ever came to defend myself, though mostly it was for exercise. However, one cannot live in such a fashion forever. People matter, Thomas. Above all else, even books, people matter.'

As each day passed more of what counts as normality in the Realm of Imagination returned. Soon enough, the subject of the children returning to the Realm of Reality came up. Councillor Gumm had already returned to the city, as had Councillor Clou, who had escaped during the attack and hidden in one of the settlements to the west of the Impossible City. Councillor Callion made a special journey from the front line in order to facilitate the children's return, but not before they held a great celebration in their honour. Councillor Gumm proposed a tremendous ceremony at the Tower of Realms, with plenty of speeches and toasts. Councillor Callion was adamant that a grand tournament was in order. It was only Councillor Clou who thought to actually ask the

176

children what they would like to do and their answer was unanimous. They felt that what everyone needed was a good party.

Every street from the Library to the Tower of Realms became the venue for this party. It reminded Thomas of the old photos he'd seen of street parties for the coronation, only this street party was altogether much more unusual. Banners of every colour were hanging from the houses. Displays of extraordinary talents could be seen, from fire-eating to juggling. Not juggling using balls, but rather a large, furry Friend juggling other Friends. It was only really now that they were allowed to mingle and talk to the citizens that it really hit home just how diverse the Friends were, and every one of them was the product of someone's imagination back in the human world.

Tables overflowing with delicious food from every culture Thomas knew about lined the streets, as well as plenty of food from cultures he didn't know about. Some of the food was edible only to certain types of Friends, but suffice to say there was something for everyone. Vibrant, lively music was played that the children had never heard before, nor were likely to hear again in their world. Everyone danced well into the evening, when the time came for fireworks more spectacular than anything seen by human eyes. Great fiery clouds of blue, green and gold lit up the sky, moving more and lingering longer than normal fireworks. It seemed a shame to Thomas and the others to have to leave this wild yet wonderful place when they'd only just begun to enjoy themselves, but they agreed that it was better to go home sooner rather than later.

The day after the party, Sylvia, who had taken a dozen very young Friends and sheltered them in a basement during the attack, came to fetch Thomas, Isaac and Emily from their rooms at the Library. The clothes they had worn the day they arrived had been washed and ironed and it was these clothes they wore for their trip to the Tower of Realms. Just as before, they met Clark and Belactacus on their way out of the Library, but this time their journey was not so rushed or secret.

'The Councillors have arranged special transportation to the tower for you,' said Belactacus as they walked out of the Library doors and out towards the street. Waiting for them was an elegant, open top silver coach without wheels that hovered over the ground. Attached to it were horses so magnificently and extravagantly patterned with bright colours you would think they'd been painted. Already inside, waiting, was Georgie. Sylvia said her goodbyes to the children here, with a great deal of hugging and fussing.

Whereas before they had travelled with the blinds down, now they rode through the streets for all to see. All around them, Friends lined the streets to cheer and wave. When they arrived at the Tower of Realms they were greeted by the remaining Councillors and shown into the very same chamber in which they had their first meeting with the Council.

'Our Explanologists have devised very sound ideas to plant into the minds of your parents,' said Councillor Gumm. 'As far as they will know, you've all spent the last week and a half as a family doing various …well, family things. Day trips out and all that.'

'We're just sorry you didn't actually get to do any of it,' said Councillor Clou.

'Oh don't worry,' said Emily. 'I think all this has been much better than any day out!'

'As soon as you arrive, the ideas will instantly appear in your parents' minds. Since they've technically forgotten you while you've been here, they'll never know you've been gone at all,' said Councillor Gumm. 'The three of us can open the portal but we'll …uh …need some help to stabilise it …'

'Emily, you're definitely more imaginative than me,' said Thomas, looking to his cousin with admiration.

'Don't sell yourself short, Thomas! You've got a fairly creative mind yourself,' said Emily, smiling. 'What will you do without the other two Councillors, after we're gone?'

'We have already begun searching for suitable candidates,' said Councillor Callion. 'Once they are chosen, the power to open the portal will be bestowed upon them. Now, the time has come for us to part ways. The people of this Realm will be forever grateful for all your help in the face of a treacherous enemy. None of you asked to be wrenched from your home and plunged into all this, but you have conducted yourselves like true heroes. We shall require a moment or two to prepare, say your goodbyes now.'

It was with an understandably heavy heart that Thomas turned to say goodbye to Belactacus and Clark. At fourteen years old, he formed opinions about people very quickly and had always felt sure that his opinions, once formed, could not be changed. In this case he was glad to find himself so very much in the wrong.

'Goodbye, Thomas,' said Clark, shaking the young boy's hand. 'Life's going to be fairly dull without you around. I might even be able to do my work without getting tackled.'

'Goodbye, Clark …and thank you again.' As Isaac stepped forward to say his goodbyes to Clark, Thomas took Belactacus by the hand.

'Clark is quite right, for once,' said the old Librarian. 'Life around here will not be the same without you.'

'I don't suppose we can …come back, ever?' asked Thomas.

'I shouldn't imagine so,' said Belactacus, who leant in closer to whisper to Thomas. 'But then again, it is not what I can imagine that matters, is it?' He winked before moving on to Isaac, who apologised profusely for his poor behaviour for about the hundredth time since Torvik's defeat. Emily hugged both Belactacus and Clark, having already said goodbye to Georgie, who had promised to take good care of Tiddles. It suddenly struck Thomas that he should say something to Georgie, but like many boys his age, the right words didn't seem to exist. Luckily for him, Georgie came up with something first.

'It's been fun, Thomas. Promise you'll think about me from time to time?'

'Y-Yeah …all the time,' said Thomas shakily.

'Well, maybe not all the time. Last thing I need is another version of me running around this Realm! Take care of yourself, ok?' She kissed him on the cheek, which naturally caught the poor young man by surprise. After one more muttered goodbye, Thomas went to join his brother, who was grinning most indecently.

All goodbyes having been said, Emily's young and creative mind was put to good use in helping the Council create a stable portal. Unlike Torvik, who had wanted to invade the human mind and exploit it, Gumm and the others were able to rely on Emily helping them voluntarily with no harm to her whatsoever. In mere moments, a stable portal had been created in the middle of the floor and unlike the others they had seen, this one was not fizzling or crackling in any way. Instead, it was a calm pond of utter darkness.

'Are you okay?' Thomas asked Emily.

'Yeah, I'm fine …I just had to imagine a sort of hand inside my mind and then I used it to …well, hold the portal steady. I also made sure it goes where we want it to. The wood just outside my house. It's going to take us home!'

'Indeed it is,' said Belactacus. 'Jump in and you shall emerge safely on the other side. Goodbye, dear friends!' With one last wave, the three children all held hands and stood at the very edge of the portal. Thomas felt Isaac's grip tighten a little, so he squeezed it gently in return. Isaac looked up at his brother. After a moment or two, he nodded, ready to make the jump. Thomas turned to Emily, who looked more than ready. Thomas counted down from three, just loud enough for the other two to hear him, and sure enough they jumped together. Just as they hit the entrance to the Void, Thomas thought he heard somebody, possibly Belactacus, call after them. By then, of course, there was no way to reply or turn back, as they had left the Realm of Imagination behind and entered the Void

180

of Nonexistence. The same numb feeling of being there but not being there came over them all, as they passed through the Void where they did not technically have form or feeling. They soon found themselves landing safely back in their own Realm, where all thought and sensation returned to their beings. The journey had been a lot smoother than the last time they traversed the Void, mostly because this time they entered it voluntarily rather than essentially being kidnapped.

The forest around them hadn't changed much while they had been gone, but then they had hardly been gone very long. The trees remained quite still this time. The weather was quite fine, just the kind of pleasant day you'd expect to find three young children out and about on. They barely heard the portal close, and only just turned around in time to see it shrink until it disappeared entirely. All around them they could hear birds, as well as a voice drifting in from somewhere nearby.

'Thomas? Isaac? Emily! Come on, you three, lunch is nearly ready!' It was Emily's mother. The three of them couldn't but laugh at the fact that they had been away all this time, had these amazing and frankly dangerous adventures, and their parents didn't have the faintest idea they had even been gone. It suddenly struck Thomas that he didn't know exactly what day trips or activities had been planted in his parent's minds, but he was sure he'd piece it together over time. They made their way back to the house together when Emily suddenly stopped.

'Did either of you catch what Belactacus said …just before we jumped?'

'No, afraid not,' said Thomas.

'I did,' said Isaac. 'At least I think I did. It sounded like … "Don't lose the pebble". I'm pretty sure that was it.'

'I wonder what that meant?' asked Emily. Isaac shrugged and resumed the walk back to the house, followed closely by Emily. Thomas stood still for a moment or two more before joining them, having stopped to check his right hand pocket. He smiled to himself when he discovered it was not empty.

Epilogue

Several months had passed since the children's adventures. Thomas, Isaac and their parents had gone back home, as one usually does at the end of a family visit. It amazed both sets of parents to see just how fond of each other their children had become during this particular visit. Naturally the children had told them nothing, but had secretly made a promise to each other to keep in touch. As Emily's parents did not own a computer, they decided they'd use a quite old fashioned form of communication known as "writing letters to each other". Isaac didn't see it catching on as a craze anytime soon. Their letters contained much about their time in the Realm of Imagination, but they were sure their parents would never get to read them and even if they did, Emily planned to claim they were exchanging ideas for a story she wanted to write. Her parents were already convinced that she would become an author someday, seeing as she read so much.

September came around as quickly as it always does to children and those mad enough to work in schools. Having recently turned eleven, Isaac was now set to join Thomas at his secondary school, a reasonably adequate facility called Pinetop Community School. All the usual fuss had been made by Thomas and Isaac's mother about buying Isaac's uniform, taking photos to send to various relatives and how grown up Isaac looked. All that and more. Considering everything he had been through just a few months ago, his first day at secondary school wasn't nearly as nerve wracking to Isaac as it might be to his classmates. In fact, he and Thomas chatted